LINGERING

CHRIS COPPEL

CRANTHORPE
—MILLNER—
PUBLISHERS

First published by Cranthorpe Millner Publishers (2022)

ISBN 978-1-80378-049-8 (Paperback)

www.cranthorpemillner.com

Cranthorpe Millner Publishers

CHAPTER 1

They knew it was the house of their dreams the moment they drove onto the property.

Tucked away amidst open fields, it could only be accessed via a narrow lane no wider than an average-sized car, lined with four-metre-high, untamed hedgerows. Driving cautiously, they had followed the twists and turns of the road until the foliage suddenly cleared, revealing a curious looking house.

It was apparent upon first glance that there was something odd about it, and as Paul scrutinised the building in more detail, he realised that it was a hodgepodge of original sixteenth century cottage combined with a myriad of extensions and modifications, the most recent addition being an extension at the back, comprising of a sitting room and kitchen, which had been carried out in the 1950s, according to the estate agent. Despite the centuries of contrasting architectural designs, there was something undeniably quaint about the place; it had a peaceful, almost comforting feel.

Even with all the extension work, it was still not what one would call a big house. It sat atop a low hill, just to the south of the village of Hurst, in Berkshire. The property came with over an acre and a half of land, a quarter of which was still forested. Only the front lawn abutting the gravel driveway, and a small, grassy rectangle that jutted out from behind the sitting room, had ever been tamed.

As they drove up to the property's gravelled forecourt, Christy squeezed Paul's hand, and he turned to see her beaming at him. Their agent, Matthew Barnes, was standing at the front door waiting for them. His shiny new Beemer was parked off to the side, allowing them to pull up right outside the front entrance.

They had been looking for the 'right' property for over a year now, though admittedly much of that time had been spent stuck in isolation, as a result of the dreadful pandemic that had swept across the planet. Even once estate agents were up and running again, it had taken Paul and Christy a good few months to pluck up the courage to start visiting properties, albeit with hand sanitiser at the ready and with masks covering their faces in an attempt to limit the spread of the virus. The 'new normal', as the scientists were calling it, did not feel normal at all.

Originally, they had assumed that their budget of seven hundred and fifty thousand pounds would be more than enough to find the perfect house, but after having seen dozens of properties within this price range, they were feeling more than a little disheartened. All the places they had looked at were either modern detached homes that were mere centimetres from the neighbours or older properties that had as much charm as toast, and they had reached a point where their rental on the Old Bath Road was starting to feel like a palace compared to what was on the market. They had always known it was going to be tough to find something within Berkshire's London commuter belt, but even so... they had expected three quarters of a million pounds to buy them something slightly more exciting than a hundred square metres of soulless red brick.

Then, as their hopes were waning, Matthew Barnes, one of the few agents who had been patient enough to continue working with Paul and Christy, had called them up out of the blue and told them that he had found their perfect house.

As Christy stepped out of their tiny Ford Fiesta onto the gravel driveway, she turned a full three hundred and sixty degrees, taking in the house and its surroundings, all the while grinning with delight. Considering they were only down the road from the M4, it was remarkably quiet, and because of the dense trees and high hedges, it was impossible to see any of the neighbours, if indeed there were any.

Paul smiled as he watched his wife pirouette joyfully on the gravel. She still had an endearing girlishness about her, and at thirty-nine, she could easily pass for twenty-five. Her naturally curly, black hair had yet to produce even one grey strand, and her love of jogging and yoga kept her looking graceful and slender.

"Mr and Mrs Chappell, good morning," Matthew greeted them cheerily. "I think you're going to like this one."

Matthew looked to be in his twenties, his boyish features hidden behind a disposable mask, and was dressed in an inexpensive off-the-rack grey suit, with a mop of hair that had clearly not seen a hairdresser's for quite some time.

"We do already," Paul replied. "Just to confirm... this is within our budget isn't it?"

"Actually, it's a few thousand under."

"Why?" Christy shot back. "With the house and land combined this must be worth at least one point two million."

"Wait until you see the inside first, then we'll have that conversation," Matthew suggested.

"Uh oh," Paul smiled. "Dead bodies and mould?"

"Nothing of the sort," Matthew replied. "Go in and have a look. I'll stay out here for distancing purposes. We can discuss everything once you've had a walk through."

Paul and Christy both produced disposable masks and white cotton gloves and put them on.

"I'd forgotten how prepared you both are," Matthew chuckled, as he stood aside and gestured for Christy and Paul to enter the house.

They found themselves in a pleasantly sized entrance hall: not too big; not too small. A cosy sitting room stood off to the right, complete with a large stone fireplace. The room's leaded windows looked out onto the front garden. Because of the low roof, they assumed that the room had most probably been used as the main sitting room when the house was originally built.

They continued through the entrance hall to the rear extension. Most modern buyers looked for sweeping, open-plan architecture, so the sitting room, dining room and kitchen of most new builds were all within one large space. But though this house had certainly been modernised to some extent, there had been no attempt to rework the interior to meet that demand. The pleasantly proportioned sitting room, which looked out onto the back stretch of lawn and the trees beyond, featured a doorway that led to what they assumed was the dining room, and this room in turn featured a doorway that opened to reveal a decent sized kitchen, complete with bountiful storage space, which greatly pleased Paul. The appliances appeared to be older, but looked perfectly serviceable. Beyond the kitchen was a utility room, and beyond that was a small shower room.

Paul and Christy walked back into the sitting room and opened another door, only to discover a narrow carpeted staircase leading upstairs to the bedrooms. Making their way up, they found clear evidence of yet more mismatched additions to the house. The narrow upstairs hallway ran for about seven metres, at which point there was a somewhat illogical step down before it continued on. The ceiling in the first part of the hall was a good height, but after the step down, the ceiling dropped, and the amount of available headroom decreased considerably. Furthermore, there was a rather precariously positioned beam just above the downward step, which any averaged sized person would undoubtably bash their head against if not paying full attention to their surroundings. Clearly the first part of the hallway was part of the later extension, whilst the low-ceilinged section was most likely part of the original sixteenth century cottage.

Lining the upstairs hallway were four bedrooms; the master bedroom was situated at the end of the corridor, in the older part of the house, whereas the other three were all in the 'newer' part. Two of these bedrooms were large enough for a queen-sized bed, but the third was so tiny it looked as though it would not even fit a small double.

Much to Christy's dismay, there was only one bathroom upstairs. It was in the newer section, and appeared to have been fully redone within the last few years. Slate grey tiles enhanced the bright white porcelain of the bathroom suite, and a large, floor to ceiling, heated, chrome towel rail occupied one of the walls. Both Paul and Christy agreed that it was a good-sized bathroom, but Christy had concerns about there being only one on the upper floor. She also made it clear that she would never use the little shower room behind the kitchen.

"Well, it's certain a quirky house," Christy stated, as they descended the concealed stairway.

"Is that good or bad?" Paul asked.

Christy stopped on the last step and looked back up at him.

"It's hard to really get a feel for the place without furniture, but I think I like it. It's funky. At some point we could convert the fourth bedroom into a second bathroom; then it would be perfect."

"What about the separate kitchen, sitting room and dining room?" Paul asked.

"I know we talked about wanting one big open space,

6

but I kind of like the cosiness of the enclosed rooms," Christy replied. "Let's face it. It's not as if we actually entertain that much anyway."

"What do you think Maggie's reaction will be?" Paul asked.

"She'll love it. There are lots of rooms; it's warm, and there's that dark forest behind the house to explore. She'll have so much more space here."

"That's true, it will take her a good few years just to piddle on all the trees!"

CHAPTER 2

After spending some time discussing the house with Matthew, they found a nearby pub so that they could both sit down and discuss what they had just seen. Because social distancing measures were still in place, the couple had no choice but to sit in the garden, the interior of the pub being too small for table service to be viable. Upon arrival, their temperatures were taken, and as a final welcoming gesture, each of them were asked to hold out their hands so that the management could anoint them with a liberal dollop of hand sanitiser.

Once seated on a rickety bench, Paul and Christy started hashing out the pros and cons of the house. There was no question that the house was not ideal, but the property's faults were almost all offset by its size and location, and privacy it afforded.

As they were waiting for their drinks to arrive, an elderly man at the nearest table called over to them.

"Couldn't help but overhear your conversation," he said, in a heavy West Country accent. "Would that be Croft House in Hurst that you're considering?"

"Actually, it is," Christy said, surprised. "You've got good ears."

"It's the only parts of me that still works."

The man's face was long and wrinkled, but distinguished, and Christy guessed that he must be in his late seventies, or thereabouts. The man's dark eyes were partially hidden by untamed eyebrows, and he was dressed in tweeds that looked outdated but in relatively good condition. Only partially covering his wispy, grey hair was a well-worn, cloth cap.

"It's a fine house," he continued.

"That's nice to hear," Paul said.

"Beautiful piece of land," the man stated, as he fiddled with the tobacco into the bowl of his churchwarden pipe.

"We thought so as well," Christy replied. "May we ask how you know the property?"

"I used to do the masonry work on that house, back in the day. There's not much of the exterior that I haven't fixed in some way. Even built a second wall up in the loft once."

"Sounds like you're the person we should be talking to," Paul smiled. "Sorry we can't have you join us because of distancing. May we buy you a drink instead?"

The man got to his feet and headed towards the garden exit.

"Not today," he said, without even looking back. "But I will say this before I go. That house... most people say it's more trouble than it's worth. You'd better decide whether Croft House is really what you're both looking for before you commit to it. I'm not saying it's a bad place. It's just not to everyone's taste."

"What do you mean?" Christy asked. "You said yourself

that it's a beautiful house."

"Aye. I did," he said, as he turned to face the pair. "It's not the house that's the problem. It's what's in it. As I said earlier, you'd best decide now whether it's worth the trouble. Once you've moved in, it'll be too late."

With that, he walked out of the pub garden. Paul ran after him, wanting to hear more about Croft House, but when he reached the car park, he could not see which way the old man had gone.

"How strange," Christy commented, when Paul reappeared.

A waitress came over to their table, placing her tray at the far end so that they could safely reach over and remove their drinks themselves. She then held out a card reader at arm's length so that Paul could stretch over and wave his debit card over the scanner.

"Excuse me?" Christy looked over at the young woman. "Who was that man sitting at the next table?"

"I'm sorry," the waitress said. "I never really noticed him. I've just come on duty. Anne must have taken his order."

"Can we speak to her?" Paul asked.

"She's off shift. She left a few minutes ago. Do you need me to ask the manager?"

"No." Christy shook her head. "It's not that important."

Once the waitress was gone, Christy turned to her husband.

"That was a little strange. Why didn't he stay for a bit and talk to us?"

Paul laughed. "This may come as huge shock to you, but

10

he may have had something better to do than natter away to us."

Christy rolled her eyes, and they resumed their discussion about the house. After a few beers, Paul was convinced that they had nothing to lose and might as well make an offer on the place. Christy, who had forgone alcohol in favour of orange juice, was less certain, and it took her a little while longer to come around to the idea.

Once they were both in agreement, Paul called Matthew from the pub garden and placed an offer of seven hundred thousand pounds. The couple had discussed going higher, but the improvements they wanted to make were likely to eat up the fifty thousand pound difference fairly quickly. Matthew sounded disappointed at the low number, but agreed to call the sellers immediately, and as Paul and Christy were heading to the pub car park, Paul's phone rang. It had been less than ten minutes.

Their offer had been accepted, on the condition that they were willing to exchange contracts within sixty days. As they were keen to move after spending so long looking for a place and had to give sixty days' notice on their rental anyway, the timing suited everyone perfectly.

The next priority was to have a surveyor do an extensive inspection of the property, to unearth anything that might be wrong. Paul and Christy were hopeful that whatever issue the old man at the pub had warned them about would be quickly detected. The last thing they wanted to do was fork out that much money for a place that would cost a small fortune to put right.

When they arrived back home, Paul emailed Matthew

their solicitor's details, then started to research the best surveyors on several trade review sites. The same name kept coming up. Wilton Chartered Surveyors, based in Maidenhead, had seemingly never had a bad review. What's more, they specialised in older homes. Paul called their number, expecting to be greeted by either a receptionist or a voicemail recording.

"Wilton Surveyor's," a young, booming male voice answered after the second ring. "Simon Wilton speaking."

"Hi there. I'm in Charvil, and have just made an offer on a house in Hurst. I need to get a survey done as quickly as possible," Paul explained.

"I've just had a cancellation for the day after tomorrow. Would that be too soon?"

"Not at all." Paul tried to keep the excitement from his voice.

"All right then," Simon continued. "I just need to run through a few questions. Do you have ten minutes?"

"Absolutely."

It took closer to twenty. Simon was very professional, describing in detail all the services he could provide. They both agreed that a full survey was needed, rather than a building-only version which, though mildly cheaper, was nowhere near as thorough. Simon had seemed intrigued when Paul told him about the age and modifications that had been made to the property during its lifetime, and was eager to take a look.

When Christy walked into Paul's makeshift office with a cup of tea, she was amazed at the progress Paul had made.

"Where's Maggie?" Paul asked, wondering why she was

not shadowing Christy as usual. The Labrador had a strange, almost obsessive adoration for his wife; from the moment they had brought Maggie home from the local rescue shelter, she had emotionally latched on to Christy, and rarely left her side.

The original reason for getting a dog was to give Paul some company while he was working from home, but instead, Maggie had become so attached to Christy that the moment she left for work each morning, Maggie would climb onto her side of the bed, snuggle into Christy's warm depression, and stay there for the rest of the day.

"I haven't been upstairs yet," Christy confessed. "Maggie. Maggie. Come on, girl."

The ceiling above them shook as forty kilos of dog bounded off the bed, and they both smiled at the amount of noise she made descending the stairs.

Maggie dived into the small living room, skidded onto the throw rug, then nudged Christy's hip while staring lovingly up into her eyes.

"Get a room, you two," Paul joked.

Maggie started to sniff Christy's legs, then her trainers. Her ears suddenly lay flat as she rested her head on her front paws, whining plaintively.

Paul looked concerned.

"It's nothing," Christy assured him. "The pub garden was full of dogs. She must be able to smell them on my clothes. I'll go change."

Sure enough, when Christy returned five minutes later in grey joggers and fuzzy slippers, Maggie reverted to her normal, exuberant self.

"Are you going to be there when they do the survey?" Christy asked.

"Absolutely. Simon insisted."

"Did you discuss distancing?"

Paul rolled his eyes. "Of course we did. We'll both be masked, and will never stand closer than two metres from each other."

Christy grinned. "Sounds like some sort of sadomasochistic recovery program."

"Where's your shadow?"

Christy looked down and was surprised to see that Maggie had disappeared. Then, they heard the floor creak upstairs. Christy called for her, but Maggie did not respond. She rattled the treat bag on the coffee table, but even that did not illicit a response.

Walking upstairs, Christy found Maggie sitting in the second bedroom, which had become Christy's study.

"What have you done?" She tried to keep the anger from her voice so as not to scare Maggie. "Paul, can you come up here please."

Paul ran upstairs and found Christy standing in the doorway to her office. The clothes she had worn to the house viewing were in a pile on the floor where she had left them. A sizeable piece of dog poo was nestled on top of them. Maggie was lying against the opposite wall, looking back at Christy with guilt-ridden eyes.

"What's going on here?" Paul asked, as gently as he could.

"I think the evidence speaks for itself?" Christy replied.

Paul knelt beside Maggie and stroked her head. At first,

she tried to back away, her eyes fearful, but slowly she relaxed, nuzzling his hand.

"She's never done that before, has she?" Paul wondered aloud, staring at the brown swirl.

"Never. I can only think that I must have picked up a bad smell in the pub garden. Maybe there was something nasty on the bench."

"Well, there's certainly something nasty on your clothes now," he joked.

Christy rolled her eyes at him, joining her husband next to Maggie and taking over stroking duty. The Labrador's big eyes looked up at her with love, but also with just the slightest trace of fear.

CHAPTER 3

Later that night, as they watched Pennywise The Clown terrorise a group of friends in the *It* movie sequel, Christy's phone rang, causing them both to jump up in shock, their nerves already frayed by the horror unfolding before them. Christy quickly grabbed her mobile and headed out of the room.

"Do you want me to pause it?" Paul shouted after her.

"God no!" she called back.

Paul continued to watch, but without Christy by his side, his bravery quickly waned, and within about five minutes he paused the movie anyway, fiddling with a Rubik's cube until Christy returned.

Ten minutes later, Christy came back, sitting down heavily on the couch. She looked pale.

"Who was that?" Paul asked.

"My father had a stroke," she stated bluntly.

"I'm not sure if I'm supposed to pretend to be sad."

"That's the problem," Christy sighed. "I feel the same way."

"Who called?"

"The woman next door who does the cleaning and cooking for him. She said he refused to stay in the hospital, and made them drive him back to his house."

"Your old house?" Paul asked in a whisper.

She nodded again.

"How bad is he?"

"His left side is paralyzed. He has trouble speaking and he can't get up the stairs."

"Who's looking after him?" Paul asked.

Christy turned to face him, her face stained with freshly shed tears.

"No," Paul said firmly. "That's not your job."

"He's still my father…"

"He stopped being your father the day he started abusing you. You haven't spoken to him in over twenty years. You have no obligation to help him now."

"There's no one else who will," Christy stated numbly. "Unless he goes into hospital, they can't look after him; there's no home care available while all these COVID variants are floating around. The neighbour has always been happy to do the cleaning and some of his meals, but I doubt she would be willing to tend to an invalid full time."

"So why does it have to fall to you? The man is a monster, Christy. The moment your mother ran off, he focused his sick, twisted mind on you. You were thirteen years old, for God's sake. As far as I'm concerned, you should let him rot in his own waste."

"You know I can't do that."

"Then we'll go down and care for him together," Paul said with resignation.

"Absolutely not," Christy shot back. "It's going to be hard enough for me to look after him; having to worry about you

17

strangling him behind my back is something I would rather not have to deal with."

"It would solve the problem, wouldn't it?" he sulked. "When are you going?"

"Babe, you know how much I don't want to do this, but I have to. He's the only family I have left."

Paul was about to interrupt but she placed a finger over his mouth.

"Please. Please can you just give me the emotional support I need right now? I'll only stay long enough to find a way to either get him into treatment or get him cared for at a nursing home."

"How long do you think that will take?"

"Maybe a week? I'll know more when I get there."

"When are you leaving?"

"First thing tomorrow."

Paul took a long breath to try and calm the anger he was feeling. He did not want Christy anywhere near the man, let alone caring for him. She had run away from home at sixteen, and had not felt the need to speak to her father since. But he knew Christy was right. She could not leave her father to die, and it would be easier for her if he stayed here. He was not sure that he would go so far as killing the old shit, but castrating him would have felt like a fair trade off.

*

The next morning, Paul waved Christy off as she turned onto the Old Bath Road heading towards Reading. During their twelve years of marriage, the couple had rarely been separated for more than a day. The prospect of Christy being gone for a week, or more, was difficult to comprehend. He had tried to be as positive as possible before she had climbed into the car to make the drive to Southampton, but inside he had been fuming, furious that Christy's father had finally found a way to bring her back home.

He tried to clear his head of the overwhelming negativity that was clouding his brain, and instead thought back to the day they had first met.

Paul had never liked crowds or overly loud music, and wasn't that into taking drugs, so when his friends had insisted that he come with them to the Isle of Wight Music Festival in 2007, he adamantly refused, that is, until he had discovered that the Rolling Stones would be headlining the three-day event. At the time, it was widely assumed that this would be one of their last gigs, after all, how much longer could a bunch of geriatric, ex-heroin addicts keep going? Paul was also curious to see Amy Winehouse. He liked her music, and some strange sixth sense told him that she was not going to be around for much longer either.

The crowds started at Waterloo station, though their drinking had begun far earlier. After a mosh pit of a train ride, the ferry crossing was even worse. The Solent was eerily calm, yet countless intoxicated music fans spent the entire journey projectile vomiting over the side railing and into the still, blue water. Once they arrived, fleets of run-down busses transported the masses to Seaclose Park, in Newport, where various colour coded camping zones had been set up.

Paul and his friends were assigned green.

The first thing Paul noticed after checking out the main stage was how bad the sound quality was, though once Amy Winehouse appeared, the quality dramatically improved. Her voice was even better live than on her CDs, though her jerky, off-rhythm body gyrations distracted him somewhat from the purity of her singing.

People were passing spliffs around freely, and Paul decided that, despite his reservations, a little cannabis might help to take his mind off the dread he felt about having to line up to use the questionable looking porta-loos. As he suspected, the drugs did the trick, and Paul drifted through the rest of the day until the sun had dipped behind the trees before setting completely, plunging the concert venue into an eerie twilight.

He had borrowed a single person tent from his dad, but even completely wasted, he didn't fancy sleeping in the thing, especially surrounded by tens of thousands of stoned, drunk fans. The tent was three inches too short for his lanky body, forcing him to sleep on his side with his legs bent, and though he had remembered the waterproof plastic to go under the sleeping bag, he had completely forgotten to bring an air mattress. Every pebble and blade of grass beneath him felt like a fist in his side, and there was almost as much noise coming from the surrounding tents as there had been from the stage.

Despite the noise, and his discomfort, Paul managed to drift into something akin to sleep, until he was swiftly woken by the sounds of a muffled disagreement, coming from the colourful tent less than a metre away from his. Paul had briefly seen the occupants before they had entered the tent to crash for the night. The man had been tall and rail thin, with his dirty blond hair tied back in a ponytail, and his girlfriend, or whatever she was to him, had a mass of wild, curly, black hair, a slender body, and gorgeous, sad looking eyes. She had reminded Paul of Monica from Friends.

Something about the girl refused to leave his stoned brain, and as the raised whispers from the neighbouring tent had slowly turned into full scale yelling, Paul tuned in to their conversation. It had quickly become apparent that the dark-haired girl had agreed to share her tent, but not her body. The bloke with the ponytail, however, was not on the same page, and no matter how many times the girl reiterated to him that sex would never be part of their relationship, the man adamantly refused to listen, continuing to berate her for not giving him what he wanted. People from the surrounding tents started shouting for the couple to shut the hell up, and Paul heard what sounded like the girl's voice being muffled. Concerned, he crawled out of his tent and stepped over to theirs.

"Miss, are you alright?" Paul asked.

"Fuck off," the man answered back.

"Miss, I need to hear that you are alright," Paul insisted.

"I said fuck off."

Paul unzipped their tent flap, but before he could look inside, a hairy leg appeared, and he received a harsh kick in the face from the man's cowboy boot. Paul was sent sprawling backwards. Stunned, he leapt to his feet, only seconds before the man emerged from the tent, wearing nothing more than a pair of grey boxer shorts and the aforementioned cowboy boots. The man's erection was clearly outlined against the thin material of his underwear.

His right hand was clasped around a chrome flick knife, the four-inch blade extended.

"I told you to fuck off. Now I'm gonna fucking do ya!" he shouted, as he took a step towards Paul.

A pair of hands emerged from the tent, grabbed the man's ponytail and pulled hard. The man screamed, causing enough of a distraction for Paul to step in, knee the man in the balls, then raise the same knee to connect with his face as he doubled over.

The girl stepped out of the tent, wearing sweatpants and bra, and picked up the knife. She then held the blade next to the man's throat.

"If you ever come near me again, I'll bloody use this."

There was something about the tone of her voice and the way she held the knife that made her threat seem completely believable.

The man gathered his few belongings and stomped off into the newly gathered crowd of onlookers, who all began to applaud, pleased with the outcome.

"You alright?" Paul asked the girl.

"Yeah. How's your face?"

Paul had completely forgotten about the impact from the cowboy boot.

"I don't know," he smiled. "How does it look?"

"A bit cheeky, but otherwise quite pleasant."

"I'm Paul," he offered, holding out his hand.

She shook it, then turned away and headed back into her tent.

"Don't I get to know your name?"

"Nope," she grinned, winking at him, before zipping up her tent.

There had been no more sleep for Paul. Thoughts of the girl bounced around his head, and he spent the night rehearsing exactly what he would say when he next saw her. It had to be funny, but still a little aloof. Cool, but amusing. Finally, as the first light of dawn crept over the horizon, he crawled out of his tent, ready with the perfect speech.

His stomach dropped.

Her tent was gone.

*

Not even watching the stage antics of Mick Jagger were enough to get her out of his head. Paul had cruised the entire venue for over two hours, trying to catch a glimpse of her, to no avail.

Eventually, Paul decided to sneak away, mid-set, and head home. Losing the mystery girl had put him in a bad mood, and he did not fancy another night in his crappy little tent. His exodus from the concert ground and the trip back across the Solent was accompanied by a cloud of misery, and once he had reached Portsmouth station, the trains were on the night schedule, so he was forced to wait on the empty platform for over an hour for the next one.

Paul was relieved to find that he had the carriage to himself, and quickly settled back into his seat and closed his eyes. He just started to drift off when he heard someone toss something in the overhead luggage rack above him. Opening his eyes, he was shocked to find the girl from the concert smiling back at him from the opposite seat.

"Hi," she said, with a huge grin. "I've been waiting for you in this bloody station for hours."

"How'd you know I'd leave the concert early?"

"I assumed you would come looking for me." She shrugged, smiling.

Paul tried to remember his ultra-cool piece of dialogue but his mind was totally blank. All he was able to do was stare at her beautiful face.

"I'm Christy, in case you're still interested."

CHAPTER 4

The drive down to Southampton took much longer than Christy had anticipated, the traffic moving at a snail's pace due to a combination of road works, an unexplained diversion, and a population who were still getting acquainted with being behind the wheel again, after months of being stuck at home.

As she neared Tennyson Road, Christy felt her palms go clammy, and by the time she pulled up in front of number 467, she felt stress chills creeping up her lower back and neck. She closed her eyes and tried to steady her breathing. As she looked at the house where she had grown up, the house in which she had been raped by her own father, she wondered why the hell she had come back. Paul had been right. Her father did not deserve the help.

She had just started to reach for the ignition key when Mrs Gillott, her father's neighbour, tapped on Christy's side window. Dragging herself away from the dark thoughts that crowded her mind, Christy got out of the car and plastered a smile on her face, hoping that Mrs Gillott would not notice the panic behind her eyes.

"I'm so happy you've come," Mrs Gillott gushed, as she backed away to a safe distance. "He's not in a good way and

I don't have the skills to properly help the poor man."

Christy did her best to keep her fake smile in place. "You've been a godsend, Mrs Gillott. I don't know what I can possibly do that you have not been doing already."

"That's sweet of you, dear, but since he had his stroke there are things he needs help with that I can't... that I won't do. It would be inappropriate. I have to consider my husband, you see. Some things are beyond what a neighbour should be doing."

Christy gave her a confused look.

"He can no longer care for himself in certain ways," Mrs Gillott explained. "He can't wash himself properly anymore, and then there's... the accidents. I have no business cleaning those parts for a man who does not belong to my family. I feel terrible for having to ask you to come all the way down here but... he is your father."

"Of course, I completely understand," Christy said, with false sincerity.

The fact was, she suddenly understood too much. When she had received the news about her father, she had not thought through what 'help' meant in the context of a stroke victim. The idea of physically cleaning her father's body after what Mrs Gillott had termed his 'accidents' made her skin crawl, and the chills crept higher up her torso. She had never for a second contemplated having to wash 'those parts' of her father. She had seen them often enough once she had turned thirteen and her mother had left the house. She sometimes still awoke screaming, remembering 'those parts' and what he had done with them.

Standing on the pavement, looking up at the front of the dilapidated terraced house, she remembered that first time, when he had promised her that all daughters let their fathers treat them that way. She had felt pain, and the heat of his body inside her. She had felt his foul, lager-laced breath on her cheek, and heard him speak the words that he would say to her every night until she had finally reached a point when she could not take it any longer.

"This is how you know daddy really loves you," he had whispered. "This is how I know you love daddy too."

Christy suddenly doubled over and brought up the bacon roll she had grabbed from the service station on her way down. Thankfully, Mrs Gillott had already gone back inside, so had not witnessed her heaving.

She straightened herself and looked back up at the grimy, grey house. A net curtain shifted on the second floor, and she saw her father's face staring back at her. His face looked distorted, though Christy could not tell whether this was because of the filthy window or the stroke. Their eyes met for a moment, and Christy was fairly certain that he was smiling.

*

Two days later, Paul met Matthew and the surveyor at Croft House. Simon was nothing like Paul had imagined him to be. The youthful voice on the phone had led Paul to expect a much younger man, but Simon was well into his fifties, bearded, bespectacled, and clad in grey trousers and a well-worn wool jacket. He wore a custom-made leather tool belt that housed multiple tape measures and a myriad of other devices that were essential to his trade.

The clouds had descended since the day Christy and Paul had first viewed the house, and without the bright, autumn sunlight, the building and landscape had taken on a monochrome blandness.

Matthew unlocked the front door and handed Simon a large bunch of keys.

"These are supposed to be for every lock in the house. Let me know if you find one without a key and I'll make sure to have a locksmith come out and make one. I have another appointment, so if you don't mind, I'll leave you to get on without me."

Simon started with the exterior, on the premise that rain might be imminent, and Paul followed him like an obedient puppy, dying to ask questions but trying to reign himself in so as not to distract the man while he was working. Simon spent most of the time on the area where the extensions met with the original building. He wanted to ensure that they had been professionally married together so that Paul and Christy would not face expensive repairs later down the line. He pointed out some dodgy flashing, some rot and weathering damage on a few of the window frames, and some pointing on the newer brick work that would need replacing, going on to explain which items would need immediate attention and which could go into a queue of things to tackle later.

After finding nothing substantial at ground level, Simon continued checking the exterior walls of the top floor while safety-strapped to an extension ladder. He made note of a few items to discuss with Paul, who was relegated to waiting at the bottom of the steps. Simon then moved on to the roof. He had warned Paul that he would be surprised if he did not find any issues between the four different roof surfaces, and Paul stood anxiously at the base of the ladder for almost half an hour, until Simon began the climb down.

"So," Paul asked, as Simon stepped back onto terra firma. "How bad was it?"

"Surprisingly, it's actually not that bad. There's a ton of little things, like bad flashing between the chimneys and the roof surface, broken roof tiles, water run-off channels that need re-tarring and so on, but nothing structural or costly. When I check the roof supports from the inside, there could still be problems, but the exterior is in fairly good shape all things considered."

Simon spent a further twenty minutes measuring every exterior wall and running a laser level across many of the newer ones.

"What's that for?" Paul asked, breaking his silence.

"I'm checking for wall tie failure," Simon explained.

Paul, having no idea what a wall tie even was, chose to wait to see if there was a problem. He stayed silent until Simon had finished his last laser measurement.

"You will be pleased to hear that your walls don't show any signs of deterioration," Simon stated, as he slipped the laser devise into one of his belt pouches.

Unlike the exterior survey, examining the interior was an endless task. Just checking every wall for damp took over ninety minutes, but though there were a few areas of concern, the house was reasonably dry and stable. In terms of electrics and plumbing, the newer additions to the house had the most issues; the older part of the house had recently been rewired, and had minimal plumbing anyway.

Simon's final target was the loft. It had expanded considerably during the building's lifetime, but Simon was pleased to see that all the roof supports had been properly and regularly treated for damp and wood worm. Simon eagerly showed Paul the hand-hewn joists in the older loft area which, though roughly cut, were in perfect condition.

"You don't know how lucky you are," Simon explained. "I fail more than fifty percent of older houses for roof supports. People never think to maintain them. This house is an exception. It's been well cared for over the years."

Simon measured all the supporting walls within the loft and entered the numbers into his iPad. A gentle beep sounded after his last entry.

"That's odd," he stated, as he stared at the screen.

Walking over to the low brick wall that supported the huge roof joists, he tapped the brick work, promptly removing a thin trowel from his belt and scraping at a few of the bricks.

"How very strange."

"What's strange? And how much will it cost me?" Paul asked, concerned.

"This wall here..." Simon tapped the wall with the trowel handle. "It doesn't align with the outside measurements."

"Let's pretend that I don't know what that means," Paul said.

Simon smiled knowingly. "Sorry. The shell, or outside measurements of the house, match all the interior walls, with a small discrepancy for wall depth, but this one here... the discrepancy is seven feet. Nobody builds a seven-foot-

"thick wall unless they're creating an underground bunker."

"Is that a problem?" Paul asked.

"Not really, it's more of a mystery. I've never encountered an anomaly like this before and to be honest I'm a little curious."

"Will I have to take down the wall?"

"Good heavens, no," Simon replied. "The structural integrity of the house is in superb shape. This wall is doing no harm whatsoever, you don't have to touch it."

"That's a relief," Paul sighed.

"I'll send you the full report tomorrow, but I can tell you right now, she's a good house. I was certain I'd find some problems on the roof but all the work that's been done to it has clearly been undertaken by professionals. It's rare to find a place like this that hasn't been damaged by over enthusiastic DIY or short cuts by cowboy builders. This house has only ever been worked on by people who knew what they were doing, and took some pride in their work."

"That's great news," Paul said with relief.

Simon was the first to descend the old loft step ladder, and Paul was about to follow him down when he felt a gust of wind swirl past him. It raised a tiny cloud of dust, which, for microsecond, stayed suspended in the air, before dropping back to the loft floor.

"There's quite a breeze up here," Paul shouted down to Simon.

"Yes, it's completely sealed. You won't get any drafts up there," Simon replied.

Paul was about to correct Simon's misunderstanding of his statement, then decided that it wasn't worth it. It would only lead to additional inspection time and all of the related costs. He opted to let it go. After all, it was most likely just a freak draft.

What harm could it do.

CHAPTER 5

Christy had spent the last hour helping her father into his cramped downstairs shower. She had picked up a plastic stool from one of the local high street shops and it quickly became a lifeline, allowing her to keep her father clean whilst retaining some distance. She would help him into the cubicle and onto the stool, then turn on the shower at only a trickle. He was then able to wash ninety percent of himself using his good arm, leaving her to finish off the parts he missed.

The 'accidents' had greatly decreased simply by getting him seated on the toilet at frequent intervals during the day, whether the need was there or not. Despite his constant protests, she would leave him alone in the loo until he was certain that there was nothing further to come. She would then settle him into the back reception room, which she had converted into his bedroom, so she did not have to help him up the narrow staircase.

Christy sipped her well-earned, daily glass of wine as she watched the BBC's evening newscast. Her phone vibrated on the stained, cigarette-scarred coffee table.

"How was your day?" Paul asked, from the comfort of their Charvil rental.

"The same," she replied half-heartedly. She knew full well that her father eavesdropped on all her conversations from the back of the house.

"I read through the survey today, all one hundred and twelve pages. I've never seen anything like it."

"Any surprises?" she asked.

"Nothing that he didn't show me at the house. It's scarier in writing though, what with all those red, yellow and green traffic signal things above each issue. There were a hell of a lot of red ones."

"I had a quick look at the copy you sent and just couldn't take it all in."

"I know. It's not an easy read. Don't worry about it, love, you've got enough on your plate down there," Paul said. "Do you want me to come down at the weekend and take you out to lunch? It would be good for you to get out of that house for a bit."

"You know I would love that, but there's no way I can leave him alone. The moment I turn my back, something happens."

"Like what?" Paul sounded concerned.

"I can't talk about it..."

"Have you found anyone who can look after him full time? It would be worth the money just to have you home."

"All the companies that offer at-home private care won't take any new clients until the New Year at the earliest. I'm still hoping to find another solution."

There was a long silence from Paul's side.

"I miss you," he finally managed to say.

"I miss you too," she replied, lowering her voice still

further.

Paul took a shaky breath, then changed the subject. "I heard from the solicitor today; he said there was a chance we could exchange within ten days."

"That's ridiculous. It usually takes sixty to ninety days at the very least."

"Apparently, because it's a bank repossession of a freehold property, they're able to move things along a bit faster. They have all the documents sitting ready to go," Paul revealed.

"Has anyone explained why the previous owner defaulted on the mortgage?" Christy asked.

"Nope. Apparently he just walked into his bank, handed over the keys and a completed deed in lieu of foreclosure, then walked right back out."

"I guess, whatever the reason, it's turned out well for us."

"It won't be long before we're sitting in that beautiful living room, looking over our own little private woodland."

"I can't wait," Christy smiled. "What about the two months' notice for the rental?"

"I spoke to the estate agent last week. We can't get out of it, but having an overlap might not be a bad thing, especially with you being down there."

"I know. The timing is dreadful."

"I don't suppose you have any idea of when you'll be back?" Paul asked.

"You know I don't."

"Is it okay if I start packing some things?"

"Be my guest. You have my full permission to pack

everything," she joked.

"If we manage to get everything sorted before you're back here, should I start moving in?"

Christy was suddenly enveloped in a wave of sadness. The idea of not moving into the new house together was almost unimaginable. That was the best part: the just-moved-in 'honeymoon' period.

"Let's talk about that once we've exchanged. Oh, speaking of which, did you tell the solicitor that I might not be able to sign the contract in person, given that I'm stuck down here?" Christy asked.

"Yes, I did. They have a branch in Southampton, apparently, so will send someone from the office to verify your ID, then they'll have you sign a copy of the contract there."

"That's a relief at least," Christy said.

There was another long pause.

"How's work? Written anything memorable?" she asked.

"Everything I write is memorable," he joked. "As I keep having to remind you, my work has probably been read more than Shakespeare. And the market for innovative Japanese technology is growing, though some of the things they come up with do seem rather unnecessary. Still, those personal sock warmer manuals won't translate themselves."

Christy rolled her eyes. "You funny man." She paused. "I have to go now. I can hear the wheelchair moving."

"You take care," Paul murmured, suddenly serious again.

"I love you," Christy replied.

"Love you too," he answered.

Ralph Burger, Christy's father, managed to slowly wheel himself into the sitting room. Christy could immediately smell shit. Despite his lopsided face, she could see that he was smiling.

"Ooo wus dat?" he slurred.

"You know perfectly well who that was. Is that why you shat yourself? Because I was speaking to my husband?"

"I uv you," Ralph said, as a trail of drool ran down the side of his mouth.

"If you loved me, you wouldn't soil yourself and make me clean you, would you?" Christy stated in a clipped tone.

Her father's smile simply widened, showing off his nicotine-stained teeth.

*

As soon as Paul had hung up on his wife, Maggie walked lethargically into his office. She stared up into Paul's eyes with a wounded, pathetic look.

"Yes, that was Christy," he confirmed.

Maggie's ears perked up at the mere mention of her name.

"You're still stuck with me I'm afraid," Paul announced.

Somehow understanding the gist of his statement, Maggie lowered herself onto the wooden floor and let out a massive sigh, placing her head on her front paws.

Looking down at her, Paul's memory flashed back to the day they had first been introduced to Maggie, at a rescue centre in the middle of nowhere, which had been highly recommended by the local vet.

They parked on the rutted concrete forecourt, before walking up to a set of buildings, surrounded by a chain link fence, and ringing a dodgy looking electric doorbell. A heavyset woman, wearing an apron over the top of worn corduroy trousers and a sweat stained t-shirt, limped out of the doorway of a temporary kennel building.

"Can I help you?" she asked, in a distinct Yorkshire accent.

"We called earlier," Christy explained. "We're here to see the Border Collie you're fostering."

"I remember. Come on through."

The woman opened the gate, standing aside to let them pass.

"She's a lovely little girl. We've had dozens of calls in the last few days since we got her."

She led them to a different temporary building, located at the back of the property. As they approached the fibreglass structure, the dogs inside had sensed their approach and had started barking frantically. Hearing the chorus of barks from dozens of different breeds, Christy and Paul smiled at one another, simultaneously wondering how so many animals had ended up at the shelter in the first place.

"We're not supposed to get too close to each other," the woman stated. "So I'll stay here at the door, and you can go in without me. You'll see the Collie at the end on the right."

Paul and Christy stepped into the building, only intensifying the din, the sound of whimpering and howling coming from the dozens of mesh cages almost unbearable.

All of them were desperate for some attention and love, and Paul and Christy were forced to look down at the floor, knowing that if they dared look at all the inmates, they would undoubtedly want to take each and every one of them home.

Reaching the end of the corridor, they turned to the right, to find an excitable Border Collie looking back at them, barking madly and running in circles around the confined kennel unit.

"I presume you know that Border Collies can be a handful?" the woman called from the other end of the building. "They were bred as working dogs and they need a hell of a lot of outdoor time to play and release some energy."

Paul shot Christy a guilty look. They had not known much about the breed at all; they had just fallen in love with the concept of having a Border Collie after having visited a working dog trial outside Henley the previous year. As they watched the Collie continue its antics unabated, they realised that the animal might just be too exhausting for them.

At that moment, something tapped Christy on her thigh. Turning swiftly, she had discovered a black paw, protruding from the next enclosure. Christy took hold of the paw and held it in her hand, meeting the eyes of the beautiful black Labrador in the cage beside the Collie. The Lab pushed her nose through a hole in the chain link, and Christy rubbed her snout with her fingers, prompting the Lab to lay down against the fence, giving Christy full access to her belly.

Paul remained oblivious, still desperately trying to calm

the Collie down enough to convince her to come to the fencing and let him stroke her.

"Babe," Christy whispered.

"Yeah?"

Paul turned to see his wife half lying on the floor, rubbing the proffered tummy of a huge black dog. The animal's large, soulful eyes were locked on Christy, and it did not take Paul long to realise that the animal had fallen for his wife. Then he noticed Christy's expression.

"So that's a no, to the Collie?" *he joked.*

Christy was too emotional to speak. All she was able to do was nod, as she stared back at the gorgeous Labrador who would soon become her constant companion.

CHAPTER 6

As the day wore on, Christy began spending more time upstairs, rather than staying in the sitting room where her father would sit and stare at her. She had naturally chosen her old bedroom as her place to sleep, but had not intended to spend her free moments up there as well, yet her father's gaze had quickly become too much for her, and she had been left with no choice but to try and spend as little time with him as possible. However, once she began using her old room as her psychological refuge, the memories of those early years came flooding back.

Little had changed. Her posters of Britney Spears and Justin Timberlake were gone, but everything else was pretty much the same. Her old CD boombox still sat on her white Argos dressing table; her paperbacks were still in the bookcase; even some of her clothing remained, which she had abandoned in favour of a quick escape.

Lying flat on her back, she looked up at the almost hypnotic Artex ceiling. Twenty years earlier, she had stared at the same raised, swirling patterns, praying to a God she no longer believed in to somehow turn back the clock to before her mother had run out on them.

Now older, wiser and more understanding of human

behaviour, Christy no longer held the same level of hatred towards her mother as she had felt in her teens, when her mother had abandoned them. She now understood the mental trauma that her father must have caused her, before he had decided to turn his 'charms' on his daughter. As a child, she had always accepted her parents' rhetoric about how clumsy her mother was. The falls... the accidents with the cooker, and the iron... the walking into doors. Now, looking back, she could not believe that she had bought the lies so completely.

She had spent the last twenty years despising her father, but still blaming her mother for the desertion. Now, for the first time, Christy allowed herself to recognise her mother's own torment. A wave of guilt washed over her, as she realised that she had blindly allowed her mother to undergo all those nightly punishments at the hands of her angry, drunk, wife-beater of a father. She could not count the number of times she had turned the boombox to full volume just to block out the sound of her father screaming at her mother over some new perceived slight.

The morning following the beatings had always played out in the exact same way. Her father would be standing in the kitchen, a jovial expression on his face, whilst her mother sat at the Formica kitchen table, nursing a black eye, a swollen lip or a burn on her arm or neck. The list of possible injuries was endless. Ralph would laugh and tell Christy how the silly cow had walked into a door or spattered herself with hot oil.

His favourite line to his wife had always been 'it's a bloody good job I love you so much; no other mug would put up with all your clumsiness, ya daft cow'.

Her mother would look up at Christy and nod in agreement, as she nursed a cold cup of tea. Her eyes had never quite been able to focus on these mornings, probably because of all the codeine and paracetamol Ralph fed her to kill the pain. It was better than having to take her to A and E, hoping that they would believe the lies.

Christy's cathartic revelation about how blameless her mother really was for all the horrors that had happened to her as a child had an unfortunate side effect: all her anger was now directed towards her father. It had been bad enough having to come down to Southampton to tend to her paedophilic, rapist father, but now, as Christy lay in her childhood bed, staring at ceiling swirls whilst reliving the innumerable nights when she had drifted off to sleep to the sound of her mother's weeping, she felt disgust rise within her. As an adult, she knew that there was no way she could have protected her mother, yet the nagging feeling that she could have done something would not leave her. It would have taken something extreme... something permanent... but still... knowing that maybe she could have ended her mother's pain was the hardest pill to swallow.

Since she had returned to the house, Christy had become more and more consumed by an anger that she could not quell, and she found herself fantasising about what she should have done twenty years earlier; about giving her father a taste of his own medicine. She saw herself pressing the old, rusted steam iron into her father's face until his flesh began to melt. Or walking his head into one of the solid oak doors, again, and again, and again, until his skull collapsed like a cracked egg.

Every time these thoughts came to her, Christy would shake them away as quickly as they had snuck into her mind, yet she was always left with the same unanswered question.

'Why didn't I just kill him back then?'

Thankfully, there was too much to do to ponder that question for too long. Between keeping the house clean and tending to her father's needs, dwelling on such impossible and unproductive fantasies was a luxury she could not afford.

The problem was, the thoughts refused to go away, playing hide and seek with her subconscious mind, waiting until she was completely unprepared before jumping out at her.

After four weeks of looking after the monster, she yet again had to help him onto the shower stool so that she could clean up another of his rare but inexplicable 'accidents'. As she held him at arm's length, closing her eyes and trying to take her thoughts away from the cramped, fiberglass shower cubicle, she felt his hand, his only working hand, reach out and move up her thigh. She assumed the action was accidental, that is, until she looked down and saw his deformed leer and his twinkling eyes.

"I stiw uv you," he whispered, as his cold fingers slid further up her leg, to where he still felt he deserved access.

Her reaction was immediate. She elbowed him in the face. Hard.

He crumpled off the stool, his body lying in a heap on the shower floor. Blood from his nose became one with the shit-stained water, and trickled down the drain.

Christy looked at him, and for a moment, she considered what she had been fantasising about upstairs. She could finish it, there and then. The problem would be solved. No one would think any the worse of her. It was not unheard of for those in his condition to slide off a stool and crack their skulls. There would not even be a court case.

Sighing, she turned off the water and walked into the sitting room, picking up her mobile and calling 999.

Within fifteen minutes, a team of paramedics arrived, and they quickly eased Christy's father out of the shower cubicle and gave him a thorough examination. Other than a possible broken nose, they could not find anything newly wrong with him. They wanted to transport him to a local hospital for a more detailed evaluation, but even with his slurred speech, he made it clear that he had no intention of letting that happen.

The paramedics spent a few minutes with both of them, outlining some safety precautions that should be put in place when an impaired individual bathed or showered. Ralph nodded solemnly as Christy asked various follow-up questions. She had no intention of changing their routine, but wanted to appear eager to ensure her father's safety.

Once the paramedics had left, Christy positioned Ralph's wheelchair so that it was facing her.

"If you ever touch me again, I will kill you," she stated flatly. Her voice was like polished steel. "Do you understand?"

He nodded.

"Do you believe me when I say that I would have no

problem doing that to you?"

Christy could see from his eyes that he did not doubt her for a second.

46

CHAPTER 7

Five weeks to the day that Paul and Christy had first viewed the property, the house purchase was completed. Paul called his wife immediately, excited to tell her that the house was finally theirs, and she seemed pleased, but distracted. She told him that she was having no luck whatsoever finding anyone willing to offer in-home care for her father. Paul urged her to consider placing him in a nursing home, but Christy, as always, rejected the idea. She knew that Ralph would refuse, making it exceedingly unlikely that anywhere would take him in.

Christy had seen the tantrums and destructive antics her father could produce when he did not get his own way. Even with only one side of his body working, he could still be one hell of a handful. Paul was fully aware of this, but Christy felt the need to remind him that patients such as her father were rarely welcomed at nursing homes, and usually ended up being carted off to psychiatric facilities.

Paul was about to suggest that this might not be such a bad alternative, but something in her tone seemed off. Unlike before, his wife seemed dead set on keeping Ralph at home. He could not be sure, but it almost sounded as though she was starting to enjoy the situation.

After hanging up the phone, Paul drove over to the estate agents and picked up the keys to their new house. He had already arranged for all the utilities when the contracts had been exchanged, so he knew that the electricity and the gas would be working. As he drove up the driveway, he could not fully believe that the house he was approaching was really theirs.

They had never lived in a place where they had not been able to hear the neighbours, and the concept of not having to share walls with anyone was an unimaginable luxury. There was nothing that upset Paul more than when his focus was broken by the sound of muffled bass coming from a neighbour's stereo or TV, whilst he was deep in the 'zone' working on his latest technical writing project. Even worse was when raised voices beyond a shared wall carried on into the night. They had once lived in what they had assumed would be a relatively soundproof flat, only to discover that they could hear every conversation, TV program and bodily function through the shared wall. One day, Christy had sneezed in the kitchen and the neighbour next door had let out a knee-jerk 'bless you' in response.

Their hatred of neighbour noise was not only limited to the inside of the house. If the weather was dry, the neighbour who had lived directly behind the place they had rented in Lincoln Gardens would religiously leave their two-year-old son alone in the garden every afternoon at two o'clock. The poor child had screamed throughout his period of banishment, the pitch of his shrieking defying distance, brick walls, double-glazed windows and doors. There had been nowhere in the house they could go to avoid the daily bombardment. Eventually, this relentless auditory assault has tipped the two of them over the edge, and they had firmly decided that the next house they bought had to be detached, and had to be distanced from the neighbours.

Pulling up to the entrance of Croft House, Paul stood for a moment, listening to the magical sound of nothingness. No loud music... no screaming children... no lawnmowers... With a sigh of contentment, Paul opened the front door and stepped into their new home. He felt a momentary pang of guilt that he was doing the 'new owner snoop' by himself, but with Christy still stuck in Southampton, he had no choice but to start the moving-in process without her. He had considered bringing Maggie, but knew that he would end up being so distracted by the dog's personal home inspection that he would not be able to focus on what needed to be done before the big move in five days' time.

Paul had a list, which would not have surprised anyone who knew him. Paul always had a list; it was his way of getting his head around any new activity or situation. Moving house to him was like a military operation. Every stage of the project had to be planned and documented. His task on that day was to work out where the usable storage spaces were, and what would go in each location.

He started with the kitchen, automatically flipping the switch that controlled the overhead lights. Nothing happened. Confused, he walked over to the hob extractor hood and switched on the fan and light. Still nothing. No electricity. Sighing, Paul silently chastised himself for not having the utilities switched over to his name the day prior to their primary move in date. When Berkshire Power had assured him that the power would be switched on any time from seven in the morning, he had hoped that they would have undertaken the task by at least mid-afternoon.

Thankfully, there was just enough light to work by, and he set about opening every drawer and cupboard, making a note of what would go in each. There was substantially more space than they needed, so deciding which cupboard would be best for what took more time than Paul had anticipated, but he wanted to get it right. Once his notes were complete, he walked around the kitchen until he found the best vantage point. As he held his phone aloft, about to take a photo, he noticed that he had left one of the drawers open. Lowering his arms, he went over and closed it, swiftly returning to his spot and taking a couple of pictures. He then walked to the other side of the kitchen and snapped a few shots from an alternate angle.

Checking through all the pictures, he was pleased with what he had captured, and was about to move on to the sitting room when something caught his eye. The same drawer was open again. Paul knew he had closed it. In fact, he had photographic proof. Just to put his mind at rest, he checked the photos again.

The drawer was open in all of the pictures.

Paul went over to it and opened and closed it numerous times. It was on gliders, and slid both ways with hardly any resistance. He closed it, then with a feathery touch, tapped the brushed chrome handle.

The drawer slid open.

Paul made a note on his iPad that he needed to fix that little problem once they had fully moved in. He had never had to deal with a drawer that was too easy to open before, but he welcomed a challenge, and was already contemplating what he might need for the project.

It took Paul more than an hour to complete his assessment of the downstairs rooms, and as the sun became concealed behind marauding storm clouds, the light within the house grew weak and insipid. Finally ready to make his way upstairs, he opened the funky door that led to the upper floor, wondering for a moment why anyone would make a staircase so secretive. Then it dawned on him. By concealing the stairs behind a door, the previous occupants had successfully prevented the living areas from being drained of warmth during the winter, as the heat from downstairs could not disperse to the upper floor. Conversely, in the summer, the door would prevent the accumulated daytime heat from rising to the bedrooms upstairs, making the hot, stuffy summer nights more bearable.

Climbing up the staircase, he was surprised to find that the fold down ladder leading up to the loft had been left extended. He had planned to save the loft till the end, but trying to walk past the ladder in the narrow hallway was a bit of a squeeze, so he decided to ascend the ladder and take a look. Poking his head into the pitch darkness of the enclosed space, he automatically fumbled for the string pull-switch that hung a few inches from his head, knowing full well that nothing would happen.

After flickering a few times, the light came on.

Paul stared up at the bulb in surprise, confused as to why this was the only light that worked, until he realised that the utility company must have finally turned on the power whilst he had been snooping around in the gloom. Relieved that the electricity had finally been sorted, he hoisted himself up and adopted the required stoop needed to navigate the low-pitched roof. He could almost stand straight if he kept to the very middle of the pitch apex, but for some reason, the plywood walkway veered off in multiple directions, none of which followed the high point of the roof. Unfortunately, stepping off the wood path was not an option, as all that stood between him and the ceilings of the rooms below was a layer of dirty-brown insulation wadding, which had supposedly been placed there in an attempt to prevent too much heat from escaping up and out through the roof.

Paul carefully measured the areas of the loft that had plywood flooring, seeing no reason why they could not be included in his storage calculations, and ultimately found himself beside the wall that the surveyor had pointed out as being somewhat anomalous. Paul noticed a set of large footprints in the dust, doubtless left there by Simon during his inspection, but just as he was about head back to the hatchway, he noticed something odd. A little farther along the mystery wall, where neither Paul nor Simon had ventured, was another set of footprints. Removing his phone from his pocket, Paul turned on the light. The prints were small, belonging to a child or a small woman perhaps, and they looked fresh.

After taking a moment to assess the scene before him, Paul came to the logical conclusion that, given the airtight nature of the loft, the footprints could have been made years before by previous occupants, and were not worth worrying about. But as he was about to turn off the phone light, a long-dormant synapse fired in his brain, and he moved the light closer to the footprints. Perfectly captured in the thin layer of timeless dust, the footprints faced the wall, and as he looked closer, he realised that they were not a complete set. One footprint was fully visible, but the other appeared to have been cut in half by the wall, with only the heel making it's mark in the dust.

Paul felt a brief chill run down his back, until it dawned on him that the wall post-dated the rest of the house, or at least, that had been Simon's conclusion. The prints must have already been there when the wall was built, in effect burying half of one shoe print. Paul had never been one to believe in ghosts and the like, but he knew Christy would get a kick out of the eerie image, so Paul snapped a close-up to send to her.

Once he had climbed back down to the upstairs landing, Paul folded up the loft steps and carried on documenting the storage space on the upper floor. Walking into the master bedroom, he flipped the light switch. Nothing happened. Frustrated, he decided that he would give the utility company a call once he had finished. They should either switch the power on or leave it off; dealing with them flicking it on one minute then off the next was infuriating.

Using the dim light filtering through the windows, Paul managed to assess the main bedroom. There was a surprisingly decent amount of storage – most unusual for an older house – and the room even had a walk-in wardrobe. On either side of the bedroom were two large, long mirrors, fixed onto opposing walls. Both were full height and adjustable, so if you stood between them, you could get a view of both your front and back. Paul's parents had owned similar mirrors, and he had spent hours as a child trying to line them up perfectly in order to create an infinity reflection, or reflective echo. By angling each mirror fractionally off centre, you could see hundreds of images of yourself, reflected in endless mirrors that curved off into the distance. Paul had spent hours fantasising about this illusion, and as a young boy with too much imagination, he had desperately wanted to step into the first reflection and find out where the curved path might lead.

Paul switched on his phone light and tried to adjust the two mirrors, but without overhead lighting, his shadow could be seen on the mirror, ruining the whole effect. He decided to wait until the power was on to try again; he could not wait to show Christy, even though he knew she would laugh and call him a nerd for being so interested in such a basic illusion.

Leaving the master bedroom, he swiftly finished his inspection of the other upstairs rooms and returned to the ground floor. His task complete, he was about to leave, when he was struck by an unwelcome thought. He knew he would feel like a complete muppet if he was right, but he had to check. Walking into the utility room off the kitchen, he opened the fuse box.

"Unbelievable," he sighed.

The house had three master breakers. All of them were in the off position.

Flipping each one, he reached over to a wall switch and

54

pressed the bottom half. The ceiling light came on. He stepped back into the kitchen and tried that one as well. The room filled with light. Shaking his head at his own stupidity for not checking the breakers first, he considered going back upstairs to play with the mirrors, but it was getting late; Maggie would need feeding soon.

Switching off the lights, he locked up the house and started down the drive, but just before reaching the street, he slammed on the brakes, struck by a deeply uncomfortable realisation. If the fuses had all been switched off, how had he been able to turn on the light in the loft?

CHAPTER 8

After so many weeks of being stuck indoors with her father, Christy was starting to develop serious cabin fever. Mrs Gillott would kindly drop by for an hour once a day so that Christy could pop down to the corner shop or nip out for a quick walk, but the other twenty-three hours she spent confined in what had been her home for the first sixteen years of her life.

The sense of imprisonment was not as bad when she was downstairs. It was the time spent in her old bedroom that was starting to take its toll, for most of the memories that she had long since buried were entombed within the four walls of what had once been a cheerfully painted room. Over time, the room had faded in her mind, making it harder and harder to recall exact details, but now that she was spending all of her 'free' time up there, her memories were slowly oozing their way back into her consciousness.

Staring up at the Artex ceiling had an almost hypnotic effect on Christy, and if she looked hard enough at one particular decorative swirl, she could feel a shift in time. The faded walls morphed back to their original colour, and Christy's fear of hearing her father's footsteps on the staircase returned as if she were a child again.

Over the past few weeks, those old emotions had been accompanied by new thoughts. Darker thoughts. 'What if?' questions that should never be imagined. She had missed the chance to punish her father back when it might have made a difference, but was it too late to take care of that final piece of housekeeping? The timing was perfect. He had already had one stroke and a bad fall... another 'accident' was all it would take...

Christy shook the thoughts away, as she had done every day since she had returned, but like losing a limb, the itch was always there, growing stronger every day. It was as if the ghost of her childhood was demanding compensation for what had befallen her in that very room.

Christy swung her legs off her old bed and took a moment to do some deep-breathing exercises. It was time to check on Ralph and make him his mid-afternoon tea, served lukewarm with a metal straw so that he could sip it with the working half of his mouth.

As soon as she reached the bottom of the staircase she could smell that he had fouled himself again, and was momentarily confused as to why he had not rung the little bicycle bell she had attached to his chair. But as she stepped into the sitting room, it became clear that he would never ring that bell again.

His head was tilted backwards, and his skin, which admittedly had never been particularly healthy looking, had turned a bluish grey colour. A thin trail of green spittle trailed from the lopsided part of his mouth, and his eyes were open, but from their opaque look, it was obvious that they could no longer see.

For a brief moment, Christy felt a red-hot rage flare up within her. After all the weeks she had spent contemplating whether to finally seek the payback she felt she deserved, the old bastard had robbed her of her chance.

She called Paul.

"I'll be there in an hour and a half," he told her.

"No. There's nothing for you to do here."

"Too late, I'm already in the car," he insisted.

"Please don't come down yet. I want to go through the house and see if there's anything I want to keep," she explained. "I never got the chance last time I left."

"I'm not going to leave you by yourself in that house with your dead father, Christy. I'm coming down and taking you out of that place, at least for the night. I'm booking the Mercure Southampton as we speak. If you want to go back tomorrow and say your final goodbyes, that's fine, but tonight, you're not going to be alone."

Christy could not help but smile. Paul somehow always knew exactly what to do. Spending the night alone in the house would have been tough, maybe even a little disturbing. Besides, the thought of spending real time away from the house made her feel almost giddy with excitement, though she could not tell whether it was just the thought of freedom that filled her with joy or the fact that her father was finally out of her life.

Picking up the phone, she called her father's doctor and told him what had happened. He expressed his regret and advised her that he would regrettably not be able to get there for at least a few hours, but Christy assured him that was fine. It was not as if either of them had anywhere else

58

to go. The doctor then went on to make a few suggestions regarding decent funeral homes in the area, and suggested that, if she felt uncomfortable seeing her father's dead body, she should camp out in another room until he arrived.

Thanking him for his advice, she hung up, and immediately contacted the first number he had given her. The nice sounding man at Lionel Webb Funeral Home promised to have a vehicle ready to collect her father the moment the doctor had confirmed his death as natural, adding that if the doctor found cause to question any aspect of her father's passing there would almost certainly be an autopsy and even possibly an inquest.

As she hung up the phone, Christy felt a sudden wave of inexplicable panic wash over her. Her father had died naturally, she knew that, but for some reason, just having fantasised about 'assisting' him with his departure made her feel strangely guilty, and the irrational part of her mind began to wonder whether just thinking those dark thoughts had hastened his demise.

Staring down at her dead father in his cheap wheelchair, she tried to feel some degree of sadness.

There was none.

Instead, all she could think about was the smell, and she promptly retrieved a sheet from the laundry hamper and draped it over him. As she cast her eyes around the room, she felt them begin to tear up, not for the loss of her father – there would never be a single tear wasted on that – but for the loss of her childhood... her innocence, whisked away like leaves in a gale.

Shifting her gaze back to the draped outline of her

father's body, she felt the darkness trapped in her soul start to dissipate. It was as if, for the first time in as long as she could remember, the sense of dread quietly lurking somewhere in the background of her psyche had stepped out of her mind. She knew that recovering would be a slow process, and that she would never be able to fully let go of what had happened to her as a child, but with her greatest fear out of her life, she had a chance; an opportunity to move on.

No more than an hour later, far sooner than expected, the doctor arrived. He was older than he had sounded on the phone, with Middle Eastern features, Christy could not help but smile to herself. Her father had been a second-generation bigot; he must have hated that the NHS had assigned him a 'damn foreigner' as his GP.

The doctor gave Ralph's body a brief examination, then turned to Christy.

"Is this how you found him?" he asked.

"Yes. I came downstairs to get him his afternoon tea and he was gone. I'm sorry about the sheet. I just..."

"Don't worry, it's understandable that you would feel uncomfortable seeing him like this."

Christy forced a weak smile.

"The stroke he had last month was very serious; he should have remained in hospital, under supervision. After suffering an incident of that severity, it is not uncommon for another to occur soon after, especially if the cause of the initial stroke has not been traced or treated. By choosing to stay at home, even with you taking care of him and with a nurse taking his vitals once a week, he somewhat condemned himself to suffering another stroke. Sadly, this one terminated his life. If it's any consolation, he would not have improved after the initial stroke; he would have spent the rest of his days paralysed and barely able to talk. I don't believe that he would have wanted that, do you?"

"No... What happens now?"

"Did you speak to one of the funeral homes?"

"Yes," Christy replied. "I called Lionel Webb. They're just waiting for your approval to collect..."

She left the sentence unfinished.

"Perfect, that will save some time. Once the death certificate is granted, you may carry out an internment or cremation. Do you happen to know which your father would have preferred?"

"I know he hated fire," she replied.

"Then your choice is clear."

The moment the doctor left the house, Christy replaced the sheet and called the funeral home. She spoke to Lionel Webb himself, and he promised to have a vehicle there within half an hour. He asked if she had given any thought towards whether her father would have preferred a burial or cremation.

"Cremation. He should definitely be cremated."

CHAPTER 9

As Christy waited for her father's empty shell to be collected, her mind took her unwillingly back to the night she had finally had enough; the night she had fled the house with nothing but the clothes on her back and the emergency twenty-pound note that she had kept safely hidden between the pages of her favourite book: Wuthering Heights.

*

She slipped out of the house before her father had even finished his supper, knowing that she had just over an hour to get as far away as possible before he climbed the stairs and made for her bedroom. She had been planning this escape for years, and having studied all her possible points of egress, she had decided that her bedroom window was the best starting point. The neighbour to the left had added an entry porch to the front of their house, and she had reasoned that its flat roof was the perfect place from which to lower herself to the ground.

With her heart beating so frantically that she feared it might escape from her chest, Christy quietly opened her bedroom window, eased out and lowered herself onto the flat roof below. The moment she felt the cracked pavement beneath her shoes, she set off in a sprint. The local streets were familiar to her, and she was confident that her father would not be able to track her down. He had always been too lazy to explore much of anything; after putting in his eight hours at the ferry dock, he was interested in nothing but drinking himself senseless, first at the Golden Sloop, then at home, where he could really focus on the task.

Darting down their street, she ducked into a pedestrian alleyway, hopped over a low wall and ran under the main road and down the poorly maintained subway that reeked of beer and urine. A pair of drunken men were standing slouched against the wall, their eyes desperately trying to focus on the young woman coming towards them.

"Oi!," one of them slurred. "Fancy a bit of fun tonight?"

"I doubt she'll be the one having the fun with your shrunken old cock," the other remarked.

Christy ignored them, making her way to the far end of the tunnel. She stopped for a moment at the base the stairs and listened for the sound of her father's footsteps running after her. There was nothing but the sound of traffic from above, and a loud belch from one of the drunken men.

Stumbling up the stairs, Christy kept running until she found herself in front of Southampton Central Station. On an inexplicable impulse, she bought herself a one-way ticket to Henley-on-Thames. She had never been there before, but she had recently seen a BBC documentary about the Regatta that took place there every year. It had looked like a safe and friendly place.

By the time she alighted from the connecting train she had caught in Twyford, it was past ten, and Henley had gone to sleep for the night. Wandering through the empty streets, she gazed into the windows of shops selling everything from stuffed teddy bears to striped blazers and straw boaters.

As a light fog slowly descended, blanketing the town in mist, Christy's biggest priority became finding somewhere to sleep. She was hardly dressed for rough sleeping, especially in damp conditions, and knew that if she did not find somewhere warm and dry, she might not last the night. As she rounded the corner of Bell Street, she came face to face with a crowd of well-to-do people, flooding out of the town's quaint theatre. Watching the predominately intoxicated audience stumble off to get behind the wheels of their Jaguar's and Range Rover's, an idea took root.

Walking over to the theatre's open doors, Christy exclaimed in a loud voice 'I think I left it under the seat', before ploughing her way through the disgorging crowd. Once inside the theatre, she broke away from the mob, and ran up a flight of carpeted steps. Her plan was simple: find a place to hide until the crowd and remaining staff were gone, and the building was secured for the night.

On one of the mezzanine levels there was a sign for the lady's restroom, and Christy promptly decided to follow it. Making her way down a narrow corridor, up a few steps, then down three more steps, she eventually came to the cloakroom and toilets. The only person up there, other than herself, was an elderly volunteer, just returning from a post-show inspection of the balcony circle. Christy quietly climbed over the cloakroom counter and hid underneath it until she was certain that the woman had left. Hardly daring to breathe, she remained in her improvised bolthole until the overhead lights had been turned off in that part of the theatre and the front doors had been locked for the night.

Christy had hoped to find some food or snacks that she could 'borrow', but the only place that might provide such treasures was the theatre bar. Unfortunately, the bar stood smack bang in the middle of the lobby, and the front lobby lights had been left on, assumedly for security reasons, illuminating the area like an airport lounge. The odds of her making it to the bar without being seen were nil.

Choosing to forget about her hunger, she decided to focus on finding a place to sleep where she would be both hidden from view and able to hear if any cleaners or staff turned up during the night. Creeping around the theatre, she managed to find an austere, windowless space just off the stage. The room looked like a manager's office, or perhaps a lead actor or actress' dressing room, and featured a sizeable sofa. Not a particularly nice one, admittedly, but preferable to sleeping on the floor.

Folding herself lengthways, Christy curled up on the stained cushions, trying to find a spot where the smell of damp was not right under her nose. From her low vantagepoint, it was possible for her to see beneath the wall mounted dressing table. A load of cardboard boxes had been piled up underneath; most of them had labels attached to them, revealing their contents to be programmes from past, present and future productions, but a few of them did not, and instead were plastered with a braded logo: 'SMITH'S'.

Christy was doubtful that she could possibly get that lucky, but just to be sure, she crawled over to the nearest box and pulled it out from under the Formica top. The box had already been opened, and the cardboard flaps dovetailed back into one another. Prying them apart, she let out a quiet gasp of delight. The box was half full of individual bags of Smith's salt and vinegar crisps. She would not go hungry after all.

Back on the sofa, having consumed three packets of crisps, her thoughts quickly became overwhelmed by an unsatiable thirst, and she began to devise the best way to sneak off to the toilets and get a drink from one of the taps. But just as she convinced herself that her plan was safe, the intensity of the evening's events caught up with her, and she promptly fallen asleep.

Her dreams were vivid and nonsensical, and during a particularly strange one where she was being chased by rabbits, after having stolen their carrots, she was roused by a stranger's voice.

"Bloody hell. We've only been invaded by rats."

Christy instantly snapped awake and practically threw herself off the sofa, landing in a heap on the cold tile floor. A young man was standing there, looking down at her.

"Where are the rats?" Christy asked anxiously.

"If I'm not mistaken, I'm looking at one right now."

Christy did not quite grasp what he was saying until it dawned on her that she was surrounded by crisp crumbs and three empty foil bags.

"Oh, you mean me," she mumbled meekly.

"That's right. I'm Brian by the way."

He held out his hand to help her get to her feet, but being stuck in the foetal position all night had played havoc with *her circulation. She stumbled into him, causing Brian to grab her arm to try and keep her upright.*

Christy looked up at him. Though a bit dishevelled and a little lanky, Brian had beautiful, kind brown eyes.

"I should go," she muttered.

"You could do that, or you could come with me to the Starbucks up the road and help me carry the crew's breakfast back here."

"What? Why would I do that?" she asked, confused.

"You look like you could use a decent meal," Brian continued, ignoring her question. "While they're putting together the order, I'll buy you a coffee and a bun or something."

Until Brian mentioned food, she had not realised how ravenous she was. She knew she ought to refuse as she could hardly expect a complete stranger to pay for her breakfast, but the thought of a hot latte and a cinnamon-raisin bun was too good to resist.

As they waited for the crew's order to be completed, Brian told her that he was one of two school interns who worked at the theatre. In return, Christy told him a half-truth: that her mother had passed away and left her penniless and homeless, unable to pay the rent. As Brian sipped on his double shot mochaccino as if it were a fine claret, a gleam suddenly appearing in his eyes.

"Fancy a job?" he suggested.

"Doing what?" she asked, hesitantly.

"The other intern decided he had better things to do than wait hand and foot on the theatre crew, so he gave in his notice a couple of nights ago. The manager was planning to

start looking for a replacement today. You're as good a candidate as anyone. Why don't I put your name forward? Say I ran into you in town and brought you back to meet him?"

"You said you were a school intern," Christy pointed out. "I don't go to school here."

"I really don't think Alex, that's the manager, will care. He needs the cheap labour."

"How cheap?"

"Three pounds fifty an hour, but if you let them, they'll work you eighty hours a week during the summer months. They pay you in cash at the end of each week, mostly so they don't have to document the fact they're probably breaking half a dozen child labour laws."

"I think they're only breaking four, actually."

Brian looked confused.

"My school teaches Law as an extra-curricular... though I guess it's not really my school anymore..."

"Oi, Brian," a barista shouted from the service counter. "You ready for this order or what?"

Amazingly, once they arrived back at the theatre, Brian managed to convince his harried manager to take Christy on immediately. By lunchtime, Christy was exhausted. In a matter of only five hours, she had painted sets, built props, stocked the bar, composed and emailed a promotional list of upcoming events, and helped Brian to unclog a toilet. She had anticipated that working in a theatre, even at intern level, would be mildly glamourous, but after spending thirty minutes trying to snake a coat hanger up and under a toilet bowl, while Brian tried to plunge the problem, any such *thoughts were flushed away.*

They had half an hour for lunch, and Brian immediately noticed that Christy had no packed meal with her. Despite Christy's objections, he approached the crew, requesting a food donation for her from whatever they'd brought with them. She was overwhelmed by the generosity of her co-workers, ending up with more food than she could possibly consume. Not wanting to appear wasteful, she squirreled away the leftovers so that she would have something to eat later that night.

After lunch, everyone set about getting the stage ready for the night's performance, and Christy and Brian were sent up to the catwalk to adjust the lights.

"Where are you going to sleep tonight?" Brian asked.

"I was hoping to give that smelly sofa another go," she replied.

"That won't work. The production crew is doing an all-night load-in for the next play."

Christy's stomach dropped; only a few coins remained in her emergency fund. The train ticket had cost more than she had anticipated.

"You can come and crash at my place," Brian offered.

A wave of panic washed over her.

"Thanks, but I'm sure I'll find somewhere."

"You won't, you know," he insisted. "At least, not somewhere safe."

Christy turned to face him head on. She only just escaped from her father's clutches and had no intention of running straight into the arms of another sexual predator.

"You've been very kind to me, but I have no intention of

sleeping with you."

Christy had expected anger or resentment, but instead, Brian laughed so hard that he almost fell off the catwalk.

"You couldn't be less my type if you tried," he managed, between guffaws of laughter.

"I'm not sure whether I should feel relived or offended."

"Don't be offended," he said. "You're actually quite pretty."

"I'm so confused..."

"I'm gay, Christy."

Christy had never felt so mortified.

"I live at home," Brian continued, saving her from her embarrassment. "But my parents are in the South of France for the week. We have a couple of guest rooms and even a washer-drier in case you need to..."

"Wash and dry?" Christy suggested.

"Yeah, that. Did you manage to bring any other clothes when you bolted?"

"How do you know I bolted?"

"It's pretty bloody obvious," Brian replied. "I mean, look at you."

Sighing, Christy shook her head.

"I thought I was going to get away with this."

"You still can," Brain told her in a stage whisper. "There's a big Tesco just down the road that stays open late. We can buy you some things to tide you over."

Christy looked at him in horror.

"I can't let you do that," she objected.

"Call it a loan," Brian replied. "You can't wear the same clothes for the whole week without someone asking questions. Besides, you're a girl. You'll need toiletries and whatnot."

Christy gave him an endearing smile. "I am running low on whatnots."

After picking up some essentials, Brian drove his Mini Cooper S out of Henley-on-Thames, towards the hills overlooking the town of Marlow. Christy expected them to keep driving until they hit a residential area, but after following the curve of the road for a while, Brian had turned down an unmarked lane, lined with solar powered lights.

"Where are we going? How far away is your house?" Christy asked, unwilling to admit that she was desperate for a wee.

"We've been on my family's property for the past minute and a half," he informed her with a smile.

Confused, and a little impressed, Christy continued to stare out of the window, until eventually, through the rows of stately cypress trees that lined the drive, she caught a glimpse of what could only be described as a mansion. Staring in awe, Christy recalled Brian mentioning that they had 'a couple' of guest rooms. Based on the outside, they had at least a hundred of them.

Parking the Mini on the vast gravel driveway, Brian entered the house through a side entrance next to the kitchen, and once Christy had visited the loo, he gave her a brief tour, before microwaving a pizza for their dinner, which they supplemented with the theatre leftovers that Christy had tucked into her jacket pockets earlier that day.

The most amazing part of the house, in Christy's opinion, was the front room, which had been converted into a luxurious office. Dark wooden bookshelves took up two of the walls, and the far one was decorated with photos, accolades and awards, all of which surrounded one of the biggest desks that Christy had ever seen. As she began to inspect the awards, she felt her entire universe start to tip and all the colour drained from her face, her knees almost buckling beneath her.

"Your father is Sir Edward Masters?" she asked in a weak, croaky voice.

Brian just grinned at her and raised his eyebrows.

"I was lecturing you on child labour laws when your father's the bloody Attorney General..."

"Shadow Attorney General. We were voted out."

"It doesn't matter. He's my absolute idol. His opinion paper on the Waymarket embargo literally changed the course of history."

"Well, if you haven't left by the weekend, you can meet him. I'm certain he'd be interested to hear about your situation."

Christy stared blankly back Brian, unable to articulate the emotions she was feeling.

Unsurprisingly, Christy was still there that weekend, and ended up making such an indelible impression on Brian's parents that a mere few weeks later, Sir Edward personally drew up a set of papers that officially transferred Christy's guardianship from her father to a trust that Sir Edward established. Her father had initially objected, claiming that he needed her help around the house, but Sir Edward had stressed upon him the fact that the only other option, considering the severity of what Christy had told him, was *to involve the police. He further stated that neither he, nor the majority of prison inmates, took kindly to paedophiles, especially those who preyed on their own children.*

Christy lived at the Marlow house until she started her undergraduate degree, studying Law at Magdalen College, Oxford. When she graduated, Sir Edward gave the Address at the University's Presentation of Graduate's event, personally presenting her with her degree certificate.

*

As she waited for Paul to arrive, Christy wondered what would have happened had she not chosen Henley-on-Thames as a spontaneous destination, or taken shelter in the historic Kenton Theatre. Without these seemingly trivial choices, she would never have met Brian, and her path would have led in a completely different direction. That reminded her, she needed to send him her latest notes on her strategy for a presentation to a new client that he was managing for her, while she was on bereavement leave. She looked at her watch. Paul would not be here for another half an hour at least. She might as well send them over now. After all, there would not be much time once they started clearing out the house.

CHAPTER 10

Much to his frustration, Paul got caught up in roadworks on the M4, just outside of Reading, and by the time he finally reached Southampton, a white unmarked van had already arrived to transport Ralph's body. Christy was in the process of ushering two sombre looking men inside the house, but as soon as she saw Paul she ran down the street to meet him, leaving the two men to do their job. The men were fast and professional. Within ten minutes, the three were in the van.

Christy asked Paul to wait outside for a moment while she dashed back into the house to grab her overnight bag. She did not want her husband's positive energy to taint the poisonous atmosphere within. She planned to wallow amongst the dark recollections stored in the brickwork until they could no longer do her any harm. Christy had always been a believer in aversion therapy as a way to break bad habits, and she fully intended to immerse herself in those memories of fear, pain and guilt until they no longer had a hold on her. By the time Paul returned to take her to the funeral, she would be able to step out of that house without any of the mental baggage she had been toting around for half her life.

As she stepped inside, she glanced over at her father's wheelchair in the sitting room. The faded NHS logo on the back seat strap was partially obscured by someone's attempt at a patch job, badly done at some point in the chair's long history. Looking at it just sitting there, Christy felt a shiver run though her body.

Returning to Paul, she welcomed his embrace as they watched the van disappear around a corner. Paul could feel his wife's stress and tension subside slightly within his arms.

Glancing up, Christy noticed something moving within the house next-door. She smiled back at Mrs Gillott, who was staring sadly out of her front window. She had been given the bad news by the doctor, who would not normally have divulged such private information, but it had quickly become clear to him that the nosy neighbour was not going to stop asking questions until someone told her what was going on. With one final nod, Mrs Gillott let the net curtain fall back in place, in effect closing that chapter of her life as well.

*

The hotel was wonderful. Social distancing was in place, of course, but knowing that their room had been cleaned with more care than at any other time in the hotel's history was not such a bad thing. They enjoyed a reasonably-priced evening meal in the hotel restaurant and, at Christy's insistence, never mentioned her father or his house once.

Instead, Paul told her about their new home, and how much nicer it was than he remembered from their viewing and the survey. Excited to show her the mysterious footprints, he brought out his phone and handed it to her, pointing at the photograph on the screen. Christy looked perplexed; all she could make out was an untouched layer of dust. Informing Paul of her confusion, he looked at the picture again and quickly realised that, even though he had been standing directly above the prints, the angle of the photograph made it difficult to see them.

"How's Maggie doing?" Christy asked, changing the subject.

"She's missed you. You'll see how much when we pick her up from the Balmfords on the way home tomorrow."

Christy took a deep breath and gently took one of Paul's hands in hers.

"I'm not going back tomorrow," she began.

"That's ridic—"

"Please let me finish," she said, patting his hand. "My father's house means more to me that you'll ever fully understand. Not in a good way, but still, it holds almost half of my life's memories. I want to clear it out, now, by myself. I need to wash away the history that remains there. I know you cannot comprehend why I would want to stay in a place where all I experienced was suffering, but please, just accept what I'm saying and trust me. When you come back down for the funeral, I'll be a new woman."

"I kind of like the old one," Paul said with a weak grin.

Christy smiled warmly. "I know. Don't you worry. I'll be the same woman, just hopefully with less darkness inside."

"I'm so sorry, love. I wish there was some way for me to take the burden from you."

"You're doing just that," she said, squeezing his hand. "You're giving me the space to do this. That means a lot."

76

Paul nodded in understanding, but Christy could tell that he was hurt by her decision.

"I'm sorry about having to leave you with all the moving-in and nesting duties," she said softly.

"Don't be. It's not as if any of this is your fault."

There was moment of silence between them.

"What about your work?" Paul asked, eventually.

"I spoke to them earlier today. Brian's fine with my leave being extended until after the funeral. I did offer to read some briefs if they needed me to, but he said that they have it covered and that I should just rest. He said I could get my head in the game once the funeral was behind me."

"You must work with the only empathetic solicitors in the UK," Paul joked.

"I know. Though I think it helps being friends with the boss."

"Can we still talk during your purgative house cleaning period?" Paul asked anxiously.

"Of course. We can talk or Zoom every day. With the house to myself, I don't have to watch what I say anymore."

"You'll miss move-in day at Croft House," Paul reminded her.

"I know, but I've got to do this."

Paul nodded again.

That night, they made love with more passion than either of them had expected. There was something cathartic about their joining that night. Christy tried to ignore the possibility that some of her frantic desire was down to her father no longer existing in this world. With his death, she felt a new sexual awakening. A freedom to give herself to her partner in a way she had never felt safe to do so before.

The next morning, after a room service breakfast, Paul dropped Christy back at 467 Tennyson Road. She felt an overwhelming sadness having to wave goodbye to him, but she knew that she had to spend this time by herself.

Stepping into the house, she immediately sensed a difference in the atmosphere. From as far back as she could remember, the house had always held an aura of fear. Whether the oppressive feeling had been forged by her mother, and later by herself, or whether it had simply been caused by her father's oppressive existence, she could not decide. But as she stood in the tiny entry hall, she could feel that some of that atmosphere had already lifted. She no longer perceived the enveloping blanket of guilt and dread that she had always felt when she stepped in from the outside.

Christy lowered herself onto the stairs and put her head in her hands, as she was overcome by waves upon waves of uncontrollable sobs. She had cried a lot in the house that had once been her home, but this was the first time those tears had been tears of relief. Taking a deep breath to try and calm her body, Christy felt the first vestiges of freedom begin to creep over the mental walls she had built as a child. One day soon, she would break down those walls, she was certain of it.

CHAPTER 11

Paul decided to try the house move without the fuss and cost of professional movers, instead making dozens of runs in his battered Honda CRV, each time packing the poor car full to the roof with boxes and personal items. For the bigger stuff, friends had recommended Tony, a 'man with a van' out of Woodley, who everyone had told them was a godsend.

Paul could now confirm that he was just that. First of all, his van was more like a small lorry, and secondly, he had arrived with one of his sons, and the two of them plus Paul had easily managed to load everything into the van in record time.

Paul had marked all the boxes with room designations, so he only had to give instructions about the placement of furniture and larger items. Somehow, the unloading process took less time than the move out, and Paul gave Tony and his son a decent tip afterwards, thanking them profusely for being so skilled at their job. The two of them seemed used to such gushing thanks, and Tony promptly reminded Paul that they were only so good at the job because it was all they ever did.

Bolstered by such philosophical logic, Paul bid them

both farewell and started unpacking. For a brief moment, he felt a pang of guilt that Maggie was again overnighting with the Balmfords, but she would have been in everyone's way during the move-in and initial unpacking. He wanted her first time in the house to be as un-stressful as possible. With the furniture in place and most of the boxes flattened and stored away, she would immediately feel at home.

Paul gently lifted the fifty-two-inch LG TV out of its box and carefully set it on the same cabinet they had used at their rental house in Charvil. Once in place, he hooked up the white cable that was lying dormant on the floor and connected it to the antenna input on the back of the TV. He had no idea whether the cable was connected to the roof antenna or if there was even any signal this far out in the countryside, but since the Sky engineer was not coming until the next day, and he had no internet until the Open Reach box was repaired – also scheduled for the following morning – this test was a critical component in his plan to spend a cosy evening in the new house watching TV and eating Indian takeout.

Switching on the TV, Paul waited. Nothing happened. There was no signal at all. Sighing, he was about to turn it off and sulk for the rest of the evening when it dawned on him that the TV had been set to HDMI 3 rather than the antenna setting before being moved. He tried again on the right input, and a pristine image of a championship darts game filled the screen.

As much as he loved television, nothing would ever convince him that watching a group of beer-bellied, white males agonising over launching a tiny projectile object at a dart board was enjoyable. The commentator referring to the players as 'athletes' somehow made the whole viewing experience even more surreal.

Switching the channel to something more bearable but equally mindless, Paul focussed on some of the more critical moving-in tasks. He began in the master bedroom, managing to eventually make the bed despite numerous protestations from both the John Lewis packaging and the fitted sheet. He then began to unpack some of their bedroom furnishings, setting a small lamp on the bedside table and filling the wardrobe with coat hangers, ready to receive their clothes.

Taking a brief ten-minute break to plug in the kettle and make himself a Roast Chicken flavoured Pot Noodle, he proceeded to work at a fairly productive pace until just past five in the afternoon. He was exhausted, but feeling positive. At least fifty percent of the boxes had been unpacked, and the kitchen boxes had all been put away, their contents having been placed in what he felt were the most logical cupboards for easy access. He knew from experience that Christy would scoff at his reasoning, and would almost certainly move everything around once she finally left Southampton, but it was a start.

Unfortunately, during the unpacking process, Paul had discovered a problem with the mobile phone reception downstairs. There was none; the only way he could get any signal was if he laid the phone on one particular window ledge. The second he picked it up, the bars dropped to zero, so he could only use it in speaker mode. Thankfully, they had ordered a Sky bundle that included a landline, so contact with the outside world would still be possible, and Paul had high hopes of finding a sweet spot upstairs, though such a search would have to wait until he had got everything else unpacked.

Tired and sweaty, he decided it was time to try out the upstairs bath and shower combo. He had turned on the hot water when he had arrived that morning, so he crossed his fingers that he would be able to have a nice hot shower, thought he was somewhat concerned that the upstairs water pressure might be non-existent, as was often the case in older houses. Still, he would never know unless he tested it.

Throwing his jeans and t-shirt into the far corner of the bedroom, where the canvas laundry basket would soon sit if he could find which box it was in, he turned on the shower. The sounds that followed were extraordinary. Paul heard the water heater in the downstairs utility room come to life with a mighty gurgle, and at the same time, the pump that was needed to pressurise the water on the upper floor sprang to life with a healthy growl. Finally, completing the raucous melody, every pipe in the house shuddered under the strain of the newly distributed water, causing air pockets to form where air pockets should never be. Paul made a mental note to bleed the system and the radiators the next day.

To his surprise, the water pressure was spectacular, so much so that he had to turn it down to little more than a dribble so that he did not splash it all across the room. He had left their cheap shower curtain in the rental with the intention of purchasing a new one, but with the move and

Christy's father's illness and subsequent death, there had not been time to choose one, so Paul was forced to shower beneath nothing more than a trickle. Fortunately, the water was delightfully hot, which was all that really mattered, and despite the meagre flow, he managed to clean all the important bits.

When he stepped out of the bath, he noticed that the mirror had only steamed up in one place, frosting over in the shape of a perfect circle in the centre of the mirror. Paul had never seen anything like it. His compulsive nature being what it was, he stood there dripping on the floor for ages, trying to fathom how the condensation had occurred with such geometric precision. It was not until he started to shiver from the cold that he gave up hypothesising.

After drying off and putting on clean jeans and a t-shirt, He made himself a strong gin and tonic, without ice or lemon. The latter would arrive in a Tesco delivery the next day, but the ice was his fault. He had been determined not to forget to bring the ice trays from the other house, and in this he had been successful, but having transported them safely to their new home, he had washed them, and foolishly left them on the draining board in the new kitchen, rather than in the freezer compartment of the fridge.

At six p.m., Paul switched the TV over to the BBC News, but after sitting through a few minutes of gloomy reports about COVID-19 and Brexit, he had seen enough. Flicking through the channels, he tried to find something more uplifting to watch, and eventually settled for a re-run of Friends on E4, which made him feel significantly more upbeat.

While half immersed in the shenanigans of Central Perk, he ordered enough Indian food from Gaylords in Twyford to feed a small army. Half an hour later, the food arrived, and Paul thanked the delivery driver warmly before carrying the heavy bag into the kitchen. The loose drawer was open again. Paul had hoped that the weight of the cutlery would have stopped it from freewheeling, but obviously that had not been enough. It was ironic really. The one drawer that opened by itself was the exact drawer he needed at this moment.

He ate twice as much as he should have, and at least three times what Christy would have permitted, but in his view a good curry called for a little overindulgence. After dinner, he poured himself a generous glass of single malt Scotch and once again flicked through the channels, and discovered that Castle Rock was on. Paul smiled to himself. A horror series inspired by Stephen King was surely the only appropriate option when spending the first night alone in an old house.

He made it through the one episode, then watched half of another, before deciding that Castle Rock was possibly just a little bit too scary for his first night alone in the house, though had Christy been here he would never have admitted being afraid. Powering up the Bluetooth speaker, he connected his iPhone.

"Hey Siri, play Imploding the Mirage by the Killers," Paul ordered.

The album started with My Own Soul's Warning, and Paul turned it up to full volume, something Christy and his neighbours would have never permitted. It was a liberating feeling, being in a house that was so detached from anywhere or anyone. He could finally play his music the way it was meant to be heard.

As he listened, focussing on Brandon Flowers' lyrics, he closed his eyes and began to doze...

Paul was standing outside Croft House, admiring the back of the property, when something caught his eye. Turning, he saw a young woman in a bright blue dress, running towards the dark void between the trees of their private little wood. She stopped and looked back at Paul. He was shocked at how pale she looked against the darkness of the trees. She stepped back into the gloom and vanished.

Paul ran after her, sensing that she was in some sort of trouble. He stopped at the tree line and tried to see beyond the gloom, but he could not make out anything but darkness. He stepped between two massive oaks and felt his way within the murk; he could sense that there was light coming from somewhere up ahead.

"Where are you?" he called out. "You don't need to be afraid. I'm here to help you."

There was no answer as he continued to grope his way towards the faint illumination. Suddenly, the trees thinned out, and he found himself less that metre away from a clearing. Parting some low branches, he stepped free of the darkness.

Shafts of dim, grey light fell onto the rich, loamy ground, piercing the greenery. At first, Paul could not make out what he was seeing. In the centre of the clearing was a single, gnarled oak tree, and surrounding it was a circle of pale, off-white orbs, protruding from the ground. As he approached, Paul discovered that the orbs were in fact mushrooms, gathered in a perfectly symmetrical circle about ten metres from the tree.

He vaguely remembered reading about mushroom circles and their mystical association with witches and fairies, but he had never seen one before. There was no doubt that their presence did add a mystical quality to the clearing, but he was not a believer in any such nonsense. He reached for his phone to take a picture, but as he looked at image the screen, he realised that the mushrooms did not look right.

Looking closer, he stared at his phone in horror. The mushrooms were gone. In their place were bones. Human bones. Hundreds of them, encircling the old tree.

Something, some sixth sense, made him look up, just as a dark object swung only inches from his head. Paul wanted to scream but he was too terrified to produce any sound. Suspended by an age-darkened rope, dozens of partially decomposed female bodies hung from the branches of the ancient oak. Their bodies danced as if operated by a puppeteer. Paul knew it had to be the wind that was buffeting the corpses, but he could not feel even the faintest breeze.

Sensing a movement by his feet, he looked down again. Something was trying to claw its way out of the dark soil.

Paul awoke with a start, his right arm involuntarily shooting out in front of him, connecting with his empty brandy glass. The glass fell off the wooden side table, and was less than a centimetre away from smashing onto the hardwood floor when it stopped in mid-air. Frozen momentarily in time, the glass gently righted itself and floated down to the floor without harm.

This time, Paul had no trouble producing a scream.

CHAPTER 12

Christy had decided to tackle one room of the Southampton house at a time, starting with hers. She was already sleeping there anyway, and had come to a sort of emotional truce with the memories held within those walls.

The bedroom only had one wardrobe, so it did not take long to sort through the dated clothing and tired selection of shoes. The only thing she found worth keeping was a woollen hat her mother had made, when she had decided to take up knitting in the hope that it would help calm her nerves. Unfortunately, the constant tick, tick, tick of the needles had irritated Ralph, and the knitting phase was quickly retired for good.

Christy carefully put aside the few items she thought might be worthy of the charity shop at the end of their street before bagging up the rest to take to the tip. She searched through the few drawers and shelves for any little trinkets that were worth saving, but after only a minimal search, she realised that she could easily survive without ever seeing any of her old possessions again.

One exception was a bright orange pottery cat that she had made at primary school for her father. Unsurprisingly, he had hated it, and had wanted it gone from the house, but Christy had rescued it from the bin, and it had lived on a shelf high above her bed ever since. Part of her yearned to take it with her to their new home, but despite the joy that had come from making it, the small, oddly shaped cat was just another link back to a time and a person that she did not want to remember.

Piling the first lot of heavy-duty waste bags in the back garden, she tried her best to fit them all into the dilapidated shed, to keep them dry and free from scavenging rodents. Returning inside, she decided to tackle Ralph's bedroom. His room was going to be the most emotionally draining to clear, but she did not want to put it off any longer. She had always been able to tear a plaster off her finger in one quick pull. She wanted to treat this room in the same way.

Retrieving a pair of bright yellow gloves and a handful of plastic bin bags from the kitchen, she strode into what had been her parent's bedroom. She had not stepped foot in this room since her mother had abandoned her; when Ralph had felt the itch to lie with his own daughter, he had always done so in her own room. Christy wondered whether this had been a deliberate choice; whether he had felt that by using her bedroom for his sick carnal needs, he could keep a clear conscience everywhere else in the house.

With almost clinical detachment, she filled bag after bag with his bedding and tired clothing. None were suitable for any future life in another household. As was the case in her room, there was only one wardrobe, but Ralph's had additional storage space above the hanging area. It was full of shoe boxes, dozens of them, yet the man had only ever owned three pairs of identical, black work boots.

Opening the boxes one by one, Christy soon discovered that they were filled with papers. She found house receipts dating back almost forty years, hundreds and hundreds of wasted lottery tickets as well as wine stained supermarket receipts. She did not even attempt to go through half of what she found in them, but in one box, tucked farther back than the rest, were a series of letters: correspondence between Ralph and her mother from their dating days. Before the time of social media, email and mobile phones, it had been the only way for lovers to communicate the things they could not express face to face.

Christy began to read, but after only a short while, she had to stop, unable to get past the grim reality that had consumed her parents earlier, heady passion. It was impossible to read how desperate her father had been to hold her mother in his arms when, years later, he had used those same arms to beat her and rape her.

She was about to give up on the contents of the shoe box when she spotted a newer looking envelope at the bottom of the pile. It was still sealed, and addressed to her. She opened it slowly, her heart racing with anxiety. It was from her mother, dated six months after she had run from the house and left Christy alone with her demented father.

For a split second, Christy considered ripping up the letter without reading it. After all, her mother's words would not change anything. The damage had already been done. But curiosity got the better of her and she removed the letter from its envelope.

My dearest wonderful Christy,

How do I even begin to put in writing what I want to say? What I feel I have to say, even if you can't bring yourself to believe my words and forgive me.

There hasn't been one second in the last six months when I have not thought of you and cried knowing what you must have thought of me. Leaving you behind broke my heart, and I need you to know that if I could have taken you with me, I would have. I hope that, when you read these words, you will understand why I did what I did.

Your father beat me on an almost nightly basis, and then, with my bruises not even fully discoloured, he would rape me, whispering his love for me into my deadened ears. This went on for over five years, and though it might have looked from the outside like I was able to cope with the pain and embarrassment of his brutalities, my mind was slowly starting to weaken, and darken.

I know that you are aware of some of the assaults he forced upon me, but there were so many that did not leave a physical mark. The scarring was internal; mental. I began to lose my clarity of thought and struggled to process even simple reasoning; I knew that one day he would strike me in just the right place and my brain would cease to function altogether. Strangely, though death was another clear possibility, the thought of complete oblivion did not seem such a bad option. Especially when the other was to become mentally childlike while your father continued to overwhelm me with his physical abuses.

I know it will seem unlikely to you, but I never planned an escape. If I had, I would have included you, and we would have run off together, at an appointed time on an appointed day. Instead, after your father held a knife to my throat while he raped me on the kitchen floor, I decided I had finally had enough. As soon as the booze knocked him unconscious, I fled, running through the streets in a frantic haze, and trying desperately to get as far away from my husband as possible.

I know that these words will be hard for you to hear, especially at your age, but I need you to know what caused me to abandon the only thing in life that I still love. I hope you understand that I had to run, and I had to run fast. I had no idea where I was going or how I would survive. The only thing I knew was that I had to leave before he killed me. Dragging you away from your home, your school and your friends would not have been fair, and sleeping rough with barely enough to eat is no existence for a thirteen-year-old girl.

I am now off the streets, living with a group of other women who have suffered in the same way as I have. I hope that the damage to my brain will recover in time, and that I will have the strength to return and take you away from that horrid little house.

I know that I have caused you pain, Christy, and I can only hope that you will one day be able to forgive me. I will understand if you do not wish to have any further contact with me, but I hope that you will allow me to still be part of your life.

It would be best if Ralph doesn't see this letter as it is meant only for you. I am sure that he has been in a miserable mood since my departure, and I am truly sorry to have left you with him. Despite everything he has done to me,

I have always trusted him when it came to your care and wellbeing. He has always loved you dearly, and I genuinely believe that he will never raise a finger to harm you. If I did not know this to be a fact, I would never have left you behind.

If you do want to see me, or even just talk to me, Mrs Gillott next door knows where I am. She also knows to only give my location to you, my sweet, sweet daughter.

I love you Christy. I am deeply sorry for what I did.

Your loving mother,
Alison

CHAPTER 13

Paul woke early and jumped into the shower, trying to shake off the strange events of the previous night. But when he stepped out and began towelling himself off, he noticed that the mirror looked different this time. Instead of one, perfect circle of misted glass, the circle was broken by two dots where the glass had failed to steam up. The dots were positioned horizontally equidistant from one another, in the top half of the sphere.

Puzzled, Paul once again tried to figure out what was triggering the anomaly, but he could not identify a rational explanation. Convinced that there must be some mystery air current that was keeping everything but the middle of the mirror free from steam, he contemplated trying to trace it, but decided to leave it for another time. He really ought to be getting on with his other household duties; there was a lot to get done before Christy came home.

Being alone had not really bothered him so far, but the concept of making breakfast without Christy felt strange. They always ate breakfast together, and used that precious time to discuss the day ahead. Feeling a pang of sadness at his wife's absence, he stepped into the kitchen, noticing that the cutlery drawer was open again, as was the cupboard above… oddly convenient given that both the cereal and bowls were stored there. Then again, after his crazy dream last night, Paul had little faith in his perceptive abilities anymore. He rarely had bad dreams, and could not think of a single time when he had endured one quite so horrific. He often had stress dreams about his writing, but they were nothing compared to last night's story line from the next *Insidious* movie.

Last night had really freaked him out; for a moment, he had genuinely believed that he was awake when the glass had executed its aerial ballet performance. It was not until he had realised that the strange phenomenon was also part of the dream that he had finally been able to calm down. He had used the nightmare as an excuse to drink another, even larger Scotch. That explained the drawer and the cabinet being open. When Paul was pissed, he always craved cereal, and judging by the biscuit crumbs on the counter, his late night fix had involved Weetabix.

Like some Pavlovian trigger, just seeing the bits on the counter caused Paul to want Weetabix again, and after drizzling on some honey and dowsing three biscuits with unsweetened almond milk, he wolfed them down as he waited for the kettle to boil. He made himself a strong instant coffee, then sat down at the dining table so he could check his messages before going to collect Maggie. He had hoped to see one from Christy, but there was nothing… either she was not awake yet, or she was busy sorting the house out. He suddenly felt a wave of longing to have her back at home. He fully understood her need to stay down in Southampton, but that did not stop him missing her.

96

Slurping up the last of his almond milk from the bowl, he washed up his few breakfast things and left them to dry on the dish rack. In all the years they had been together, they had never used a dishwasher; for just the two of them, it was more of a pain to load it, run it and unload it than it was to wash everything up by hand.

Realising the time, Paul grabbed his keys, and was about to step outside when he noticed that his umbrella was lying on the floor. It must have fallen during the night. Picking it up, he stood it back in the corner and opened the front door. It was tipping it down. Sighing, he stepped back into the hallway, grabbed the brolly, and made a dash for the car.

Maggie was so happy to see him, she could hardly control herself. She did her iconic sideways shuffle, a couple of full circles, and for the grand finale she rolled onto her back, her belly pointing to the sky. After giving her copious belly rubs, and profusely thanking her carers, Paul loaded Maggie into the back of the car and headed back to their new home.

*

Christy just sat there. She had read the letter twice more, and found her brain to be in some sort of vapor lock. She could not seem to connect the words to her feelings. She was stunned to find out that her mother had tried to contact her. The worst part was knowing that, by not responding to the letter she had never received, she had given her mother the impression that she did not want to open any lines of communication.

Twenty years had passed, during which time memories

of her mother had been tainted, not just by the abandonment, but also by her mother never having attempted to reach out to her. Christy had let the initial anger fester and take root, blaming everything on her mother. Now, in one letter, she had discovered that not only had her mother tried to speak to her, but that she had also only left her because she believed Christy to be in safe hands.

Christy could feel the mental walls that she had erected over the past twenty years beginning to crack, compromising their protective capabilities. She instantly folded the letter and gently placed it into the back pocket of her jeans, setting the thoughts that had come with it aside.

Unlike the letter from her mother, she treated her father's detritus with little respect, not caring whether she damaged or even destroyed the clutter that filled his room. Roughly shoving all his clothes, papers and other items into plastic bin bags, she lugged them all downstairs, ready to be taken to the tip and purged from existence.

*

Paul opened the front door to the new house, allowing Maggie go in first. He had little choice. She had been pulling on her lead all the way from the car, and the second he had opened the door she had almost pulled his arm off, such was her excitement to explore her new home.

Having been released from her lead, the Labrador charged through the entry hall and into the sitting room. Plenty of serious sniffing took place, but nothing seemed worthy of additional exploration. She then dashed through the sitting room, again without bothering to stop for a more in-depth investigation, but once she reached the utility room, her sniffing became more focused.

She quickly discovered the cupboard where both her wet and dry food were stored, and she promptly stood next to it, looking up at Paul as if to say, 'it's not doing much good shut in there, is it?'. Paul smiled, leading her over to the opposite wall where her two food bowls and her water feeder were already full, awaiting her pleasure. She took a single bite from each, but was too excited to stay still long enough to eat anymore.

Returning to the sitting room, Maggie went straight to the stairway door, much to Paul's amazement. How she knew that the door led to the stairs was beyond him. She gently pawed it until Paul swung it open, and swiftly bounded upstairs, taking the steps three at a time. She ran feverishly through the bedrooms and the bathroom, then finally came to a dead stop beneath the loft hatchway. Lowering herself to the floor, she whined plaintively as she stared up at the square hatch.

"Not a chance, old girl," Paul informed her. "It's got a ladder and you know how much you hate those."

She cocked her head as if considering his statement, then rested it back on her paws. Paul tried to persuade her to come downstairs with him, but she remained stubbornly where she was.

Paul shrugged.

"Well, you know where I am when you want some company."

He headed down to the sitting room, expecting Maggie

to follow.

She did not.

Paul started working on unpacking the boxes labelled 'misc. docs'. They were filled with everything from warranties and manuals to yellow legal pads, filled with dozens of false starts at novels that he had begun and then tossed aside.

As he tried to decide where to distribute the various bits of paper, the doorbell sounded, and Paul almost jumped out of his seat in surprise. Opening the door, he discovered a grumpy Open Reach technician, who after exchanging some brief pleasantries with Paul went straight over to the junction box and rolled his eyes.

"You've got a mark one," he mumbled. "No wonder it's not working. These were unreliable when new."

Paul had no idea how to respond, so he offered the man a cup of tea instead.

"Milk, no sugar, please," came the reply, as the technician began to remove the notorious mark one unit.

Paul walked into the kitchen and filled the kettle, turning to grab a mug and a teabag from the cupboard. As he turned, the cupboard door opened by itself. No longer surprised by this strangely common occurrence, Paul made a mental note to check whether the units on that side of the kitchen had been misaligned, or attached to a sloping wall. Either would be a suitable explanation for the kitchen's self-opening drawers and cupboards.

By the time Paul appeared with a mug of tea, the technician had removed the old box and was wiring in the new one. Paul placed the cup next to man and was rewarded with what sounded like a growl, but may well have been a thank you. Half an hour later, he watched the man plug in the Sky Hub box. Less than a minute later, Paul was able to connect his iPad to the internet.

Life was grand.

The rest of the day was spent sorting the contents from the last few boxes, before Paul tackled the task he had been looking forward to the most: positioning and hanging their art collection, as Christy liked to call it. It was hardly a collection. It was more of a random group of posters, paintings and photographs that they had either created themselves or had found at local art fairs and charity shops. The entire 'collection' was probably worth less that a meal at the pub, but they loved it.

Paul believed himself to be an inspired picture hanger; he felt he had the gift for finding exactly the right spot for each piece of artwork, and Christy always sensibly agreed with his positionings. However, unbeknownst to Paul, over a period usually stretching between four and six months, his wife would subtly move one piece at a time to a more suitable location. She did it so stealthily, and over such a long period of time, that Paul had yet to catch on to her, and she fully intended to keep things that way.

Paul was about to hang up a tiny oil painting of a wine cork that they had bought at a pub auction, when the doorbell rang again. The Sky engineer had arrived, wearing a mask, a face shield, nitrile gloves and rubber boots. From what Paul could make out, he was a heavyset, bald man in his forties. His name tag said 'Erwin'.

Paul showed him where the downstairs TV was located,

then led him to the master bedroom and pointed to where he hoped Christy would permit a second TV. She had never been sold on having a television in the bedroom, but Paul was determined to persist.

Walking back outside, they surveyed the exterior of the house, and the engineer spotted a now useless first-generation Sky dish attached to the roof. He spent the next hour removing it, and installing a new smaller version. That task completed, he ran a cable from the dish to a spot on the outside wall, closest to where the sitting room TV was located, using a massive drill bit to pierce through the brickwork like a knife through butter. He also drilled a hole up in the loft so that he could feed a cable through to the proposed upstairs TV.

Returning inside, he carefully reattached the Sky box that Paul had carried over from the old address, then spoke to the Sky control centre to get the box reactivated at the new location. Fifteen minutes later, the Sky Q home-screen appeared, and Paul knew that normality had been restored.

Leading the engineer upstairs, Paul found Maggie still lying under the loft entrance. She usually went completely giddy when a new human entered the house, but she hardly gave the man a second look, and it took both of them to gently push her aside so Paul could lower the folding stepladder.

As soon as Paul opened the hatch, Maggie went nuts, howling up at the opening like it was the end of the world. Paul had only ever seen Maggie howl once, when Christy had put on an Alanis Morissette album – something about the singer's voice seemed to resonate with the Labrador.

Erwin gave Paul a concerned look.

"Is there something about your loft you need to tell me about?" he asked.

"Not a thing. I don't know what's wrong with her... she must be going crazy because she can't get up there and have a snoop. She's only been in the house a few hours."

Erwin did not fully buy Paul's story, but he climbed up anyway. Paul left him to it and returned downstairs, leaving Maggie on patrol under the hatch. Paul was playing with the Sky remote when the engineer came down the stairs. He looked dusty and slightly dishevelled.

"You've got a problem," he stated. "I can't run a cable to the bedroom."

"Why? The loft's empty. It should be easy," Paul replied.

"Should be... yeah. But there's this wall that shouldn't be there. I fed fifty metres of cable into the loft from outside and now it's all stuck behind that bloody wall."

"Couldn't you remove a few bricks just to grab the cable?"

"Not without your permission," Erwin replied.

"Consider it given," Paul said. "It's not a load bearing wall, is it?"

"No. It's only attached to the joists and roof by some L brackets."

"Then do whatever you have to do," Paul instructed.

The man nodded and headed back up the ladder, after carefully stepping over the Labrador. He knelt by the mystery wall and tapped it in a few places, trying to gauge a weak spot. He decided to try and remove one brick from the bottom row. That way he could use one of his cable grabbers to snag a loop of the cable he had threaded into the house from the outside.

Using one of his flat head screwdrivers as a chisel, he began to gently tap away at the mortar between the target brick and those surrounding it. It was slow work, but he was making progress, and with one final tap, he knocked away the last bit of grey mortar from above the brick. Searching through his tool bag, he found the flat piece of wood he usually used to protect flooring when he had to solder wires, and laid it flat against the brick. He tapped it hard with a rubber headed hammer; the brick shifted a millimetre. He gave it a second whack, and the brick was released, vanishing into the wall.

Proud of his accomplishment, Erwin fed his longest cable grabber all the way into the void. He had no way of seeing what he was doing, so he had to judge everything entirely by feel. He slid the long wire with the tiny, hooked end in and out of the hole until he felt it come into contact with something on the floor. He wiggled it in a few different directions and confirmed that whatever it was, it was able to be moved. He made a few attempts at hooking it with the grabber until, on the fourth try, it snagged. He gently pulled the grabber out of the hole and saw a brand-new length of black cable trapped in the hook.

Erwin pulled the cable until it would not budge, then began to gather it up, intending to take it down to the other end of the loft and feed it through a hole into the bedroom. But as he it started to coil the cable, it began to retreat back into the wall. Erwin grabbed it and gave it a good hard pull. Something pulled back. He assumed it was stuck on some old piece of construction detritus, so he pulled harder. The cable snapped out of his hands and vanished into the hole.

Erwin stepped away from the wall. He knew that the cable was not stuck on anything. Something was pulling it back, and whatever it was, it was strong. He turned back to his tool bag, to see whether he could figure out a different tactic, and saw that a large box of black cable clips had fallen out of his bag and spilled across the dusty loft floor. He was about to gather them up when he realised that they seemed to have fallen in some sort of pattern. Turning on his torch, he quickly realised that it was more than just an orderly spill. The black cable clips had come together to form two words.

HELP ME.

Unaware of what was going on upstairs, Paul was channel surfing, and had just started watching a terrible, low budget movie on the Sci-Fi channel. But when Paul heard Erwin running down the stairs, he stood up, surprised by the speed at which the engineer was moving. He was even more surprised when the man burst through the door and practically sprinted through the house and out of the front door, barely acknowledging Paul.

"Hey? Have you finished?" Paul called after him.

The engineer ignored Paul and threw his kit into the back of his brightly branded van. Paul caught up with him just as Erwin was jumping into the driver's seat.

"What's going on?" Paul asked.

Erwin turned to face him. His mask was askew, and his skin was white as milk. He also seemed to be shaking.

"No cable for the bedroom. Sorry."

Erwin slammed the door and started the engine, accelerating down to the end of the drive, as if he was not aware of the T junction it formed with the narrow lane. Somehow, he made the turn, and before Paul could really process what had just happened, he was gone.

Hearing Maggie barking like a lunatic inside, Paul walked back into the house and up the stairs. He found her at the base of the folding stepladder with her front paws on one of the rungs, baying up at the loft.

"Good grief, dopey girl. What's wrong with you?" He patted her head but she did not seem to notice.

Gently pushing her aside, Paul climbed up and into the loft space. He ducked down and crab-walked over to the wall, wondering what on Earth had upset the man. He could not see anything amiss. One of the bricks had neatly been removed, and it looked like the bloke from Sky had made a valiant attempt to retrieve the cable, apparently to no avail. Shame really, even the house seemed to be against him having a TV in their bedroom.

Looking down, Paul spotted a load of cable clips scattered on the floor, and he picked one up to inspect it. They were decent cable ties, the ones that were always sold out in B&Q. Paul grinned. There might be an upside to the engineer's sudden and unexplained departure.

CHAPTER 14

The days passed quickly, with Christy tackling the house room by room, and after almost a week of clearing, she arranged for a consignment furniture seller to collect whatever items she thought might have resale potential. He was a jovial young man, and kindly gave her the number of a friend of his who owned a large van, telling her that he would happily take the rest to the dump for a small fee.

That same day, Christy received a call from the funeral home. The certificate had been overnighted directly to them, meaning they could now schedule the funeral. Lionel Webb stopped by the house later that afternoon, taking out an expansive catalogue and showing Christy all the funeral options that were available to 'enhance the final departure of her loved one'.

Christy explained, with minimal detail, that her father was not a loved one, and that she wanted the bare minimum when it came to the service, the casket and whatever else was essentially required. Mr Webb showed her a coloured brochure with page after page of shiny and expensive caskets, hoping that he might be able to sway her, but Christy was adamant; she saw no reason why she should pay thousands of pounds for a polished wooden box that was only there to suspend the body while it burned to nothing but ash. Asking him what was used when the state had to pay for a cremation, he explained that they used a heavy weight industrial cardboard. She smiled, and told him that she would have one of those.

In a last attempt to upsell his client, Mr Webb pointed out that an industrial carboard coffin would not look very appealing during the funeral service. Christy, who had just about had enough of the funeral director, stepped into the other room and returned with the sheet she had used to cover her father's corpse while waiting for the doctor to arrive.

"Cover it with this."

*

Paul was busy working on his latest translation project when his phone rang. It was Christy, telling him that the funeral was booked for Friday, in two days' time. Paul sighed with relief. She would finally be coming home.

After expressing his relief to Christy, and asking her for the details, they went on to talk about how she was coping, and what clothes and shoes he should bring for her to wear for the service. He also asked if she wanted him to come down the night before, so that they could be together the night before the funeral, but unsurprisingly, her answer was no. She wanted to be alone that night so she could say her final goodbyes to the house.

The funeral was scheduled for eleven o'clock, so they agreed that Paul should arrive a couple of hours beforehand so that Christy could get dressed in plenty of time. Given that they were Ralph's only next of kin, they reasoned that they ought to be at the crematorium at least half an hour before the service began.

With plans for the funeral sorted, they caught up on what they had both been up to since they had last spoken, and Christy laughed aloud at Paul's description of Maggie's goofy behaviour.

"She's going to be one happy dog when you get home," he said.

"What about you?" Christy asked.

"I'm going to be one happy man."

*

Christy met with her father's solicitor the following day, dreading the possibility that he might have left her the horrid little house in his will. The office was a modern building, only a few hundred metres from one of the larger marinas. The moment she approached the reception desk, she was handed a blue face mask in a sealed bag, which she promptly put on, pointlessly smiling at the masked receptionist.

Christy could not help but notice that the girl's mask was the re-usable type, imprinted with the company logo. She could not decide whether such branding was clever or coldly opportunistic. They had found a way to turn the unwitting employee into a walking advertisement.

The receptionist pointed towards the waiting room and apologised for not being able to offer her coffee or tea, citing COVID as the reason. Christy would have passed on both anyway. She wanted to get the whole process over and done with as quickly as possible; she hated the fact that she would more than likely have to go through the entire probate process just to have the government take forty percent of whatever her father had left behind. Then there was the ordeal of trying to sell the house and having to deal with months of endless buyer queries. She just wanted to get the funeral behind her and walk away from everything to do with her departed father.

An immaculately dressed man in his fifties stepped into the waiting area and walked up to her. He was wearing the same branded mask.

"Mrs Chappell," he said, in a very posh voice. "I'm Richard Peele."

Christy stood and almost reached out to shake his hand, before remembering that physical contact with strangers was a thing of the past.

Richard led her to his comfortably furnished office and offered her a chair, positioned a good distance away from his desk.

"Your father revised his will a few months before his... illness. Were you aware of the codicil within the later document?"

"I was not," she stated bluntly.

"Well," Richard continued. "It's a very straightforward estate, and the probate should go through without much fuss."

He opened a leather folder on his desk, ready to read the document within.

"Before you start," Christy interrupted. "Do you mind just telling me what he left. I don't really care about all the legalese. I'm a solicitor myself; I could recite most of that document to you by heart."

Richard did not seem the least bit fazed.

"He's left you sufficient funds to cover the cost of the funeral, and has bequeathed you his car."

Christy sat, waiting for the rest, then realised that Richard had finished. There was no 'rest'.

"Car?" she said, confused. "I didn't know he even had a car."

"Apparently he did. It says here that it is a 1996 Ford Escort Estate. I will provide you with the garage location, the parking receipt and the keys whenever you're ready, though I must warn you that the vehicle will be listed as part of his probated assets."

Christy burst out laughing. He had left her the same old car he had owned before her mother had run away.

"That's it?" she asked.

"Yes, I'm afraid so. I am in no doubt that you must be terribly upset about not having been left the bulk of his estate, but I must tell you that it is not unusual for a beneficiary to be changed this late in the day."

"Actually, I'm delighted. I really didn't want anything from him. You've just made my day."

"That's certainly not the reaction I was expecting."

"May I ask who the rest of the estate went to?"

"As the other beneficiary would normally have been present today, were it not for these strange times, I see no harm in telling you, especially as she was here yesterday to receive her reading of the will. Everything else went to a Mrs Henrietta Gillott. I believe she was your father's next-door neighbour, and helped him a great deal in his later years."

"Did she know that she was in the will?" Christy asked.

"Apparently not. Indeed, she was somewhat distressed by the news. She was concerned about what her husband might think; I believe she feared that he might suspect more was going on between her and your father than a little cleaning and the occasion meal being prepared."

If Mr Peele had been able to see through the triple layered disposable mask, he would have seen Christy grinning from ear to ear.

As she was about to exit the office, Mr Peele called after her.

"Mrs Chappell, you've forgotten the keys to the car."

"No, I haven't."

*

Paul had slept incredibly well that night, and needed a long, hot shower to wake him from his dozy state. Feeling invigorated, he stepped out of the bathtub, and turned to face the mirror. The same fogged circle with two equidistant clear dots stared back at him. Used to this phenomenon, he lathered his face with shaving cream, then reached for his razor. But when he looked back at the mirror, he saw a third dot, positioned in the lower half of the circle on the right side.

Paul shrugged, and was about to draw the disposable razor across his cheek when he saw that the new dot was moving. He stepped back from the mirror and watched as the condensation disappeared in the shape of curved line, drawn from right to left with the two ends being the highest points of the curve. It took Paul a moment to realise what he was seeing.

Something had just drawn a smiley face on the mirror.

In a complete panic, Paul tried to wipe it off with his towel, whilst simultaneously standing as far from the reflective surface as possible. He desperately wanted to run out of the room, but for some reason, he could not move. He was completely terrified, but at the same time, his obsessive-compulsive side wanted to know what had drawn the face, and how.

Cautiously stepping towards the mirror, he blew hot air onto the surface and fogged up the mirror in a different place, then drew a circle. He stood back and waited for something to happen.

Nothing.

He added a smile.

A few seconds later, two dots appeared.

"Who are you?" Paul asked the empty room.

He waited, but there was no answer. He tried the fogging test again, but his half-drawn smiley face remained incomplete. Still feeling on edge, he finished shaving and brushing his teeth, all the while glancing around the room, expecting some other inexplicable event to occur.

As he walked out of the bedroom, he saw that Maggie was still under the loft hatch, even though Paul had retracted the steps, closing access to the room above.

"Come on girl, you're losing it. Let's get you some breakfast and I'll take you on a walk."

She looked up with big sad eyes, but refused to budge. Sighing, Paul gently took hold of her collar and led her downstairs. Once they entered the utility room, Maggie became her usual self, leaning against him as he opened her dedicated food cabinet and watching intently as he emptied a packet of wet food into her bowl. Before he could even place it on the floor, Maggie had her muzzle in it, and she had licked the bowl clean by the time he placed some dry food next to her.

Relived to see Maggie restored, Paul stepped into the kitchen, just in time to see the cutlery drawer and cereal cabinet open by themselves. He stopped in his tracks. He was starting to understand that whatever it was that was playing with him, it was not remotely malicious. In fact, if anything, it appeared rather good natured.

He took a deep breath, then walked over to the countertop, closing the drawer and the cabinet door and backing away.

"Okay, you've got my attention. Let me see you do it again."

Paul stood and waited for something to happen. After almost ten minutes, he grew bored of waiting and opened the fridge to retrieve the almond milk. As he turned back to the countertop, he saw that both the drawer and cabinet were once again wide open.

"That's not clever," he stated, as he studied the cereal collection lined up like books in the cupboard. He was about to reach for the box of corn flakes when the box of frosted shredded wheat beside it slid towards him. His felt the hairs rise on the back of his neck, but at the same time, he found the interaction strangely amusing. What made it stranger still was that he found himself preferring the idea of frosted shredded wheat over boring old corn flakes.

Halfway through his bowl of cereal, he heard the kettle

switch on, and he somehow knew that it was so he could make his cup of morning coffee. He shook his head at the bizarre occurrences that were transpiring within their new home. His thoughts then drifted to Christy's return the next day, and to what her reaction to the extra house guest was likely to be.

The full weight of the situation came crashing down on him.

"Oh shit. I've got to tell Christy that we've got a bloody ghost."

Maggie strolled up next to Paul and laid her head in his lap. He stroked her behind the ears until something distracted her. Walking about a metre and a half away from where Paul was sitting, Maggie suddenly sat down. Moments later, she held out a paw, then, seconds later, she rolled over. Paul stared at her in confusion. Maggie was going through her repertoire of tricks... tricks that she only performed on command. But Paul had not said a word.

He stared at the Labrador as she sat on her haunches and began to beg in the middle of the room, facing a blank wall. Her tongue was hanging to the side, as her eyes stayed locked on something that only she could see.

It was clear to Paul that she was waiting for the next command.

But from who?

CHAPTER 15

Christy woke up for the last time in her childhood bedroom. It felt strange… not only would she never see it again, but its time capsule quality would also be erased, and no doubt replaced by something less personal and more befitting of the times.

She was not remotely sad to think of it being transformed into someone else's room; someone who would imprint their own memories. Hopefully happier ones. Christy wondered if any of the room's tainted history would ever find its way through the new wallpaper and paint. Would a child sit in that same room in the future and suddenly feel an inexplicable sense of fear and despair?

She hoped not. It was nicer to think that, by the simple act of changing hands and applying a new décor, years of horror could disappear without leaving any trace.

Walking through the house one last time, Christy again felt a rush of relief, knowing that she would not have to deal with it ever again. The previous night, she had searched deep within herself to see whether she felt even the slightest hint of jealousy towards Mrs Gillott. There was none to be found. If anything, she felt happy and relieved that the sweet woman next door had received a well-deserved reward for looking after her unpleasant and demanding neighbour for so many years.

Christy locked the back door and checked all the downstairs windows. She had already dropped a set of keys through Mrs Gillott's letter box, and for a moment, had considered ringing the bell. She wanted to let her know that there were no hard feelings over the bequest, and that Christy and Paul wished her great success with whatever she chose to do with the house. Then there was the other reason for speaking to her. The letter had said that Mrs Gillott had her mother's address, if ever Christy intended to get in touch with her.

Part of her wanted very much to speak to her mother, but another, the stronger half, felt that maybe it was best to leave things as they were. What if she did try to contact her, only to find that her mother no longer wished to communicate, or worse, had herself passed away. Christy did not feel up to dealing with such a psychological rollercoaster.

As she was putting one last bag of rubbish into the council issued black bin, Paul pulled up in front of the house. Stepping out of the car, dressed in his best black suit, he retrieved her Hawaiian, flower-motif overnight bag and walked towards her. Christy smiled. He looked so handsome all dressed up like that, and as he came within her reach, she held out her arms towards him, pulling him into a tight embrace.

"Do you want me to wait out here?" Paul asked after a moment, pulling away slightly.

"No. I'm done with the house. Why don't you come

upstairs and keep me company while I get dressed? You can tell me everything you've been up to in our new home."

Paul smiled, hoping that she could not read the thoughts that were buzzing around his head. Now was not the time to discuss their potential ghost situation.

Once Christy was dressed, the pair spent a few moments giving the house a final once over, before stepping out onto the pavement. Christy double checked that her Fiesta was locked.

"When is my car being picked up?" she asked.

"They said they'd pick it up by noon tomorrow."

"Good. I'll need it for work the next day."

Christy was about to get into Paul's car when she stopped, turning to take one last look at her childhood home.

"Saying goodbye?" Paul asked.

"More like good riddance," she replied, as she climbed into the passenger seat.

Half an hour later, Christy was staring out of the car window as they neared the crematorium. The last puzzle-shaped gaps of blue sky were being swept away by dense, moody clouds, heavy with rain. Paul felt that the sombre skies were perfectly fitting for such a day.

The first thing Christy noticed as they stepped into the small chapel was that there were pitifully few mourners. She had contacted everyone from her father's old, leather address book, but had been unable to find any trace of a digital version on his ancient desktop computer.

There were nine masked people in the chapel, including the clergyman, and Christy was surprised to see that the coffin, which sat to the right of the pulpit, was draped with the sheet she had handed to the funeral director. She had expected him to take her command as nothing more than an irrational quip from someone suffering the stress of her loss, but apparently he had taken her seriously. Perhaps it had not been as bizarre a request as she had thought.

The service was brief and surprisingly unemotional. Strangely, even without knowing the true history of the man in the cardboard box, the minister gave none of the usual over-the-top, aspirational synopses of her father's life. Christy was beyond relieved. To have been forced to sit there and endure him being praised as a fine humanitarian and doting father would have been too much.

After a recording of 'Be Still for the Presence of the Lord' had been played over the speaker system, the box and sheet began moving along a conveyor belt, between a pair of dark green velvet curtains. The progress of the coffin was slow and reverent; the sheet getting caught up in the curtain material, less so. Eventually, the cardboard coffin vanished from view, leaving the ugly sheet in a pile on the conveyor belt. Something about the imagery made Christy want to smile, but in an astonishing display of self-restraint, she kept her funereal expression intact the whole time.

Slowly, the chapel emptied, with each mourner being greeted by the minister with an elbow bump instead of the usual handshake. As Christy and Paul thanked him for the wonderful service, Christy noticed a masked woman heading towards her, with an older man in tow. When the couple were three metres away, Mrs Gillott lowered her mask to reveal her identity, not that Christy had been in any doubt.

"I just wanted to say that I hope you're not angry about the house and everything." Mrs Gillott sounded deeply concerned.

"Not at all," Christy replied. "In fact, I'm delighted. You helped him so much over the years; I think we both know which one of us deserved that windfall."

Much to Christy's shock, Mrs Gillott started to cry, and before she could process what was happening, the woman refitted her mask and stepped towards Christy, enveloping her a strong hug.

With her masked face near Christy's shoulder, she whispered, "We both know who deserved the most after the horrors they had to endure all those years ago."

Sobbing, Mrs Gillott stepped away, making sure there was no touching of skin.

Halfway back to the car, Christy heard rather than felt something in her jacket pocket. Intrigued, she reached inside and removed a folded envelope, yellow with age. Christy did not have to open it. She knew exactly what the other woman had slipped into her pocket.

"Everything alright?" Paul asked.

"Yeah. Just thinking, that's all."

"I thought there was something different about you," he joked.

"Prat," she replied.

"Seriously though, how are you feeling? This has to be a very surreal day for you?"

"That's putting it mildly."

A rumble of thunder sounded in the distance.

"Is that your stomach?" Paul asked.

She playfully punched him in the arm.

"Why don't we stop at the Cricketers on the way home?" he suggested.

"I'm not sure I'm that hungry."

They reached the car, and Paul held the passenger door open for her.

"I have one thing to say to you."

"What?" she asked.

"Banana bread pudding and whiskey cream sauce," he answered, as if in passing.

"Oh my God. I'd forgotten about that. We haven't been there in ages. Maybe we should stop by just to make sure they're still in business."

"They were when I called this morning and booked a table," Paul stated proudly.

Christy shook her head and smiled. She was feeling a little better already. In fact, she was feeling more than just better. She felt great. Probably not something to boast about after one's father's funeral, but then again, he had hardly been what most would consider to be a stable parent.

Because of the M4 road works around Reading, Paul decided to take the M3 the whole way from Southampton, turning off at the Bracknell exit. Not only was it a faster route, but it also, by happy coincidence, brought them out a few miles short of Warfield and the Cricketers Inn.

Paul had chosen the Cricketers because it held nothing but good memories for the both of them. It would help to take Christy's mind of the funeral, and hopefully give him a chance to mention some of the surprise goings on at their new home.

The recently renovated dining room was socially distanced, oddly giving it a cosier feel than when all the tables had been in place, and Christy's earlier lack of appetite vanished as soon as they sat down, as did any semblance of her normally health-conscious diet. Paul stuck to ginger beer, but Christy managed to down two glasses of Chardonnay and was feeling no pain. Instead of their usual practice of sharing a dessert, Christy insisted that they each had their own.

Paul was within a microsecond of bringing up the exciting news about their mysterious house guest when the manager stopped by to say hello. Paul and Christy had been regulars before the full lockdown and had built up a great relationship with her, so she was delighted to see them both. They spent the next fifteen minutes catching up and hearing all about the drama from the early days of COVID, including staff shortages, client complaints and issues with the brewery supply chain. But the manager assured them that things were finally getting back into a routine now, which she was most relieved about.

Once she was gone, Paul was again about to bring up the topic of the day when their waitress, wearing a mask and face shield, delivered another ginger beer for Paul and a third wine for Christy. She made all sorts of remarks about how she really shouldn't, and how she would be pissed off her face if she drank the whole glass, before proceeding to essentially neck the whole thing.

Almost prophetically, Christy did end up pissed off her

face. Her coordination became iffy, her eyes glazed over, and she suddenly felt the need to sing the jingle from the old Cadbury's Fruit and Nut commercial.

"Everyone's a fruit and nut case..." she slurred.

The waitress returned with a card scanner and Paul quickly wafted two credit cards over the reader so that he could pay less than £45 on each of them and thus avoid having to touch any of the buttons on the credit card verification device.

He tried to be discrete as he led his wife out of the restaurant, but Christy kept waving her hands in the air and shouting theatrically 'goodbye you lovely people. I look forward to seeing you all again very, very soon. You've been a lovely audience. Truly lovely'.

Paul finally got her to the car, at which point she fell asleep, her head leaning against the passenger window. Somewhat frustrated that he had missed the opportunity to break the news about their helpful house guest, he hoped that she would be in a better position to deal with that conversation once they had reached Croft House and she had slept off the alcohol. The last thing he wanted was for her to experience the ghost's actions without having been warned about the spectre first.

CHAPTER 16

By the time they got home, Christy was awake, but drunkenly intense. She told Paul how much she loved him approximately twelve times between the Sonning roundabout and the house, and as he helped her out of the car, she stood swaying, staring up at their new home in awe.

"It's so beautiful," she slurred. "Can we keep it? Oh, please let me keep it. It's so pretty."

Paul put his arm around her and steered her gently towards the front door.

"It's yours. You can keep it for as long as you want."

"Really? I love you Paul Chappell."

The moment they walked into the entry hallway they heard a commotion coming from somewhere above them. Maggie came flying down the stairs and was so frantic to get to Christy that she could not get proper traction on the hardwood floor. For a split second she seemed to be doing an impression of a cartoon dog running in place, until her paws finally found some grip, and she propelled herself towards Christy. In a move worthy of an Olympic gymnast, Maggie managed to somehow flip onto her back before even reaching her best friend, sliding the last few feet with her belly in the air.

As Christy stroked her, Maggie wriggled with unbridled happiness and joy.

"She's missed you," Paul said, stating the obvious.

"Ditto," Christy replied, then hiccupped.

"Come on, let's get you to bed."

Paul took her arm and helped her to straighten up, walking her though the sitting room and up the stairway. Other than an initial misstep at the bottom of the stairs, Christy managed to get the rest of the way up with some degree of dignity. Considering that Maggie was thigh bumping her the whole way, Paul was amazed that she made it up at all.

He tried to convince Christy to change into something less formal than the dark suit she had worn at the funeral, but she crawled under the duvet fully dressed, right down to her Harvey Nick's shoes. She was asleep before Paul could even make another comment.

Being boringly sober himself, he decided to use the bonus time to catch up on his latest work assignment from Mashihoto Electrics. They were about to launch a new type of hair trimmer and needed him to create the wording for the manual.

*

Mashihoto had first become aware of Paul when he had been working in London for the marketing giant Grant Davis, during which time they had assigned him the job of junior product editor for their account. After only a few weeks, the company noticed Paul's flair for being able to make even the most mundane item sound interesting, and thus essential, and they quickly stole him away from Grant

125

Davis and brought him and Christy to Tokyo, so that Paul could learn not just the product line, but also the philosophy of the company as whole. Christy had at first been reticent to take a sabbatical from her solicitor's job, but rapidly accepted the choice as being one of the most rewarding decisions she had ever made.

Paul and Christy had never seen anything like Tokyo, and while Paul was working, Christy would head off and explore new neighbourhoods and suburbs, until she knew the city better that some of the locals.

A few months into his new job, during a strategic launch meeting for a newly invented laser head massager, Paul had the audacity to criticize the wording and tone of Mashihoto's instruction manuals. Despite Mashihoto being one of the world leaders in consumer electronics, Paul argued that they could get an even higher market share penetration if they changed one simple thing. The manual. He pitched that every electronics manufacturer used the same mundane, dry language to explain the proper use and care of their product. Because of this, hardly any consumer read those instructions, preferring to either give the manual a cursory glance and access the most basic functionality of the product or fiddle with the item until they got it to work.

Paul had suggested that creating engaging manuals would improve user experience, as consumers would not only use the product to its full potential, but would also engage in its other capabilities, meaning they would enjoy the product more and would therefore be more likely to choose Mashihoto for their next product.

After the meeting, Paul was called to Miru Mashihoto's

office on the top floor of the building. Miru had been educated at Harvard University, and spoke perfect, unaccented English. He listened carefully as Paul outlined both his idea and a simple means of testing it. Miru gladly approved the test, and gave Paul free reign to work with the technology group to create his own instruction booklet for the company's latest product: a miniature 'bird's egg' speaker.

The reactions of consumers and technology reviewers was immediate. They loved it. Not only was the manual completely user friendly and highly informative, but it also led the reader down an intuitive exploration of all the product's functions. The writing blended humour, technology, and easy to remember steps in order to walk the new user through every piece of knowledge they needed to fully enjoy their new gadget. When the full reviews of the product came out, it did not go unnoticed by Miru that the manual itself had received almost as much review space as the baby speakers themselves.

From that day on, Paul became responsible for every product manual, and after almost a year of working in Tokyo, he convinced Miru to allow him to continue his work from the UK. Miru had given him a six-month 'trial' contract to work remotely, and eleven years later, Paul was still their lead writer, despite living on the other side of the planet.

Thinking back on it now, it seemed crazy to Paul that he had managed to land himself the perfect job, especially now, with working from home becoming the norm rather than a rarity. Leaning back in his seat, Paul felt tightness in his back, and realised that he has been working for four hours straight without a break. Stretching slowly, he unkinked his body before going upstairs to check on Christy.

She was awake, lying on her back and staring at the ceiling. Maggie was lying next to her, stretched out to almost his wife's full length.

"I think I got hit by a bus," she announced in a croaky voice.

"I think it's more likely to be the bottle of wine you drank with lunch," he suggested.

"I only had two glasses. That's not enough to make me feel like this."

"You had three 250ml glasses. A bottle holds 750ml. You do the maths."

"But I only had two," she insisted.

"Don't you remember the manager sending out another glass for you?" he asked.

She shook her head.

"Do you remember singing the fruit and nut song as you left the restaurant?"

She shook her head again, looking horrified.

"What about running naked around the car park, you must remember that?"

Christy's eyes opened as wide as a pair of saucers.

"Okay, I might have made up the last part," Paul chuckled. "Here's an idea. The shower is fantastic. Why don't you use up all our hot water and stand under it for as long as you can?"

"Only if you get me two paracetamol and glass of water. With ice."

Paul went down to the kitchen, closed the open cutlery drawer and cereal cupboard, and filled a glass with cold water and a few cubes of ice from the freezer. Grabbing the paracetamol from one of the drawers, he took the pills upstairs. With great effort, Christy managed to swing her legs out of bed, and taking the two pills from Paul she placed them in her mouth one at a time and swallowed, grimacing as she washed them down with the icy water.

Shivering, she was about to flop back down on the bed when Paul helped her to her feet.

"Shower first," he said, smiling.

"Where's my dressing gown?"

"On the back of the bathroom door."

"And my makeup?" she asked.

"In your case, I would imagine," Paul said, as he pointed to the brightly coloured suitcase parked outside the walk-in wardrobe.

"And my kiss?" She offered her puckered lips.

Paul smiled, kissing her gently, before walking her towards the shower.

"Don't forget to undress before you get in," he called after her once she had closed the bathroom door.

After receiving an unintelligible reply from Christy, which had most likely involved at least one expletive, Paul looked over at Maggie. She was still passed out on the bed. Paul leaned over and whispered in her ear.

"Din dins."

After taking a moment to untangle herself from the bedding, Maggie shot out of the room and bounded down the stairs. Paul smiled to himself as he followed her in a more sedate manner.

After watching Maggie devour her evening meal, he opened the back door to see if she would go out on her own yet. She sat on her haunches and looked up at him as if he were completely insane. To be fair, Paul had not yet had the time to give her a full tour of the grounds and teach her where she could and could not go. Passing beyond the front hedge onto the street was the perfect example of no-go territory.

Paul threw on his coat and grabbed her lead, prompting Maggie to jump in circles with uncontrollable excitement at the idea of walkies. It was already starting to get dark, so Paul hoped she would settle for a perfunctory walk that night. He would take her for a serious exploration of the neighbourhood the following day.

Paul headed towards their personal area of woodland, with the intention of only going as far as the tree line. The darkness within the packed trees looked blacker and more eerie than Paul felt it should. Then again, he knew that there was nothing there but trees. Anything more was coming from his own imagination.

Maggie unexpectedly started to pull frantically on the lead. She seemed to want to go inside the copse of trees. Paul tried to hold her back, but he was no match for the overexcited dog, and before he knew it, she had pulled him beyond the tree line into a darker, quieter place. There was no sound except for the rustling of leaves and Maggie's panting.

Paul suddenly recognised where he was; this place was identical to the place he had seen in his dream the other night. He forced himself to calm his breathing. It had only been a dream. This was reality. He was simply walking his dog through their beautiful, wooded garden.

Maggie stopped and began to sniff the ground, following the scent for another few metres, before running through some overgrown brambles, dragging Paul behind her. They emerged in a small clearing, where an ancient-looking oak tree stood in the centre of a perfect ring of mushrooms.

Paul, in a burst of superhuman strength, picked Maggie up into his arms and staggered out of the woods with as much haste as he could muster. Once they were far enough from the dark trees, he placed her back on the ground and walked her in tight circles around the perimeter of the house, until she had done her business and Paul had got his heartbeat back under control.

Opening the utility room door, he heard Christy shouting from upstairs, but he was too far away to hear her clearly, so he removed Maggie's lead and walked through the kitchen, closing the cutlery drawer on the way. He started to head up the stairs, but heard the familiar sound of Maggie trying to open an unattended bag of dry food with her nose. Paul realised he had forgotten to put it back in the cupboard.

"Just a second," he shouted upstairs.

"What?" Christy called back.

Paul quickly removed the kibble bag from Maggie's evil clutches and shut it in the designated cupboard. He patted her on the head and looked into her pathetic eyes.

"I know. We starve and torture you every day."

He then headed back to the bottom of the stairs.

"I couldn't hear you before," Paul yelled.

"You've got to come and see this," Christy yelled back.

Paul felt like he had just swallowed a lead ball. The hairs on his neck had also risen to the occasion.

"The mirror's fogged up in a perfect circle. It's got two dots in it."

Paul ran up the stairs, hoping to get her out of the bathroom before anything else happened.

Christy's scream reverberated through the entire house. She had just met the ghost.

CHAPTER 17

Paul ran into the bathroom and found Christy backed against the tiled wall, staring blankly at the smiling image in the mirror. He grabbed a towel and wiped it away with one sweep, then stepped in front of her and took her head in his hands.

"It's nothing," he said, with complete calm.

Christy's eyes started to focus. She looked around herself as if surprised at where she was. Then she looked at the mirror.

"Something drew a face on the mirror," she stated.

"It's nothing... really."

"Don't tell me it's nothing," Christy replied. "I just watched something invisible draw a smiley face on the bloody mirror. The one thing it's not is nothing."

"Okay," he said soothingly, as he tried to hug her. "It's possible that we may have a..."

"A what?" she interrupted, pushing him away.

Paul drew a deep breath.

"A ghost, maybe," he offered.

"Maybe!?" she seethed. "I've been in this bathroom, naked and alone, and you knew that we had a potential poltergeist creeping around the place?"

"I don't think it's a poltergeist. She seems completely benign," he argued.

"She, is it? You've seen her then, I take it? What the hell have you been up to while I've been gone?"

"I haven't seen her... or it. I just get the feeling it's a she."

"Oh, please, do tell me more about this feeling," Christy said sarcastically.

"I just think that she's a she, that's all," Paul said, shrugging.

"Why?"

Paul had to choose his next words carefully.

"She seems to be most active in the kitchen... so, naturally, I assumed..."

"Do you have any idea how sexist you are sounding right now?" she asked angrily.

"If you plan on being angry, you should probably focus on the haunting instead of my political correctness, don't you think?"

Christy's glare softened.

"You're probably right," she said, her voice gentler now. "Go on then, tell me about this new friend of yours."

They moved to the bedroom and perched on the end of the bed as Paul told her everything that had gone on during her absence. Well, almost everything. He decided that she did not need to hear about his nightmare concerning the woods and the mushroom circle.

"And you didn't think to mention any of this to me?" Christy asked, once he had finished.

"To be fair, I only knew for certain that we had an issue yesterday morning."

"You really thought that the drawer opening by itself and the kettle turning itself on whenever you fancied a hot drink didn't count as red flags?"

"I was still mulling those things over. I wasn't sure what was causing them."

Christy shook her head in disbelief.

"I only knew for sure when I got the smiley face treatment that you just had," he stressed.

"That must be her big party trick," Christy said flippantly.

"So, what do you want to do?" he asked.

"I would suggest we get someone in, wouldn't you?"

"Someone? What, like a priest?" he asked.

"That's for exorcisms. There are people who can speak to spirits and make them go away. There was that place on the news the other day, the one in Lewes. You should try calling them."

"Surely we must be able to find someone more local? I'd feel like a complete muppet, calling some stranger and telling them that we need ghost abatement."

"It's their job, I doubt they would think you even remotely silly," Christy said. "But you raise a good point. It might be best to keep the whole thing more local. After all, ghosts don't improve resale value. I wonder whether Margaret would be able to help? If I remember correctly, she did some training a while back, just after they bought their house. One of the upstairs rooms had an eerie feel to it, so Margaret employed this medium to come in, and they completely cleared the air. She was so impressed that she decided to learn more about it. I have no idea how good she is, but it might be worth a try."

"So, which of us gets the honour of calling her and having to listen to half an hour's worth of local gossip?" Paul asked.

One look at Christy's expression was enough to let him know who was going to be the lucky lottery winner. Paul felt that Christy was blaming him for their ghost situation, which he did not think was remotely fair, and he also struggled to understand why she wanted to get rid of it before they knew anything about the spirit.

Paul managed to coax Christy downstairs for some toast and a cup of tea, and once he had put the kettle on, he began searching for the pot of Marmite. He knew which cabinet it was in, but he had not quite got around to sorting the contents of each shelf into some sort of sensible order.

Christy walked in while he was elbow deep in tea bags, condiments and sweeteners, feeling around for the glass jar.

"For someone as methodical as you are, you're not very good at organising cupboards, are you?"

"No, my darling. Then again, even if I had spent any real time on it, you would have just reorganised it anyway."

"Good point."

Exhausted by her husband's chaotic searching, Christy grabbed her mug of tea and wandered into the sitting room, whilst Paul continued to hunt for the Marmite. Eventually, he found the syrupy goo that Christy loved so much, and forced a mound of it to adhere to some buttered toast. Once the snack had been ceremoniously delivered, Paul returned to the kitchen to retrieve a tea for himself, leaving Christy to fiddle with the Sky remote.

"Stupid piece of tech... why can't I ever get this thing to work properly?" Christy grumbled, taking a sip of her camomile tea.

Grimacing at the blandness of it, she was about to ask Paul if he would add a little honey, when her attention was grabbed by the TV. The picture now only filled half the screen, and there were English subtitles running along the bottom.

"Paul? I've messed up the tellie again," she called out.

Paul appeared and gaped at the screen.

"I don't know how you always manage to do this. I've shown you how to go back and undo your actions."

"I wish that worked on you," she said tartly, pointing the remote at Paul.

He took it from her and started to calmly go through the various settings, ignoring his wife's penetrating stare. Realising that Paul might be there for a while, Christy accepted that she would have to add the honey to her tea herself, so she headed back into the kitchen, opening the cabinet.

"Paul!" she exclaimed. "Get in here."

Paul walked in and gave her a curious look.

"What's wrong?"

Christy pointed to the inside of the cabinet. It was immaculately laid out, with everything correctly grouped and visible. All tall items were at the back, with the smaller ones in the front.

"Look what it just did!" Christy exclaimed.

Paul looked back at her and grinned sheepishly.

"You're just miffed because she did a better job than you

would have done," he said.

Christy gave him her glare of death, then reached in and grabbed the honey. As she turned to the cutlery drawer, it opened by itself.

"You're going to call Margaret first thing in the morning and get this house cleansed."

Christy stormed back into the sitting room.

"Don't you think you're overreacting just a little? It's obvious that she's a nice ghost. Maybe we should see how things progress as we get to know each other better..."

"Tomorrow, first thing," Christy yelled from the other room.

Paul knew she was right, but he also felt that the spirit had more right to be there than they did. After all, she had clearly been there first; in a weird way, they were the interlopers. Then again, he knew that Christy would not permit any sexual activity until the occupancy count went back down to just the two of them and Maggie. Getting rid of the ghost was the only way forward if he wanted to preserve their relationship.

"How did you manage to fix the television so fast?" Christy asked.

Paul was about to tell her that he had not actually worked out how to fix it yet, but for his own self-preservation, he thought it best to keep that to himself.

"It's a guy thing," he joked. "You just have to know what buttons to press."

The open cutlery drawer slammed shut behind him.

"If guys knew which buttons to press, we wouldn't need vibrators," Christy called out.

Paul got the distinct feeling that neither woman had appreciated his button comment.

Joining his wife in the sitting room, the couple watched a few old episodes of Below Decks Caribbean, and after an hour or so, Paul could see that Christy was starting to fall asleep again. He was about to turn off the TV when he had an idea.

"Honey, watch this," Paul said, almost proudly. "I know you think that the ghost isn't doing any good here, but wait till you see this."

Christy gave him a doubting look. Paul placed his water glass on the side table and gentle pushed it to the edge. He looked up to make sure she was watching then gave it a light shove. It somersaulted over the edge and smashed onto the hard wooden floor.

"Wow, that was definitely worth waiting for," she said, as if she was talking to a small child. "You must have worked so hard every night trying to figure out how to break one of our best glasses."

Paul just sat there as Christy bent over and kissed him on the head, before heading back up to bed with her cup of tea.

"When you've cleaned that up, don't forget to take Mags for a walk."

"I already did, just before you woke up from your meganap. By the way, where is she? I haven't seen her in a while."

"She's under the loft hatch, and is refusing to leave. Any idea what that's about?"

"Not a clue," he replied flatly.

Christy shook her head and made for the stairs.

Once Paul had heard Christy's footsteps pass overhead, he whispered, "You could have caught it like you did with the brandy glass."

He looked down at the remains of the fine crystal, and was about to get up and search for the brush and pan, when a tiny light appeared among the shards. Fascinated, Paul watched on in complete awe as a glowing mist began to encircle the debris, and the bits of glass rose a few inches above the floor, seeking out others of their kind. In a mesmerising swirl of shards, the broken glass reassembled itself, then slowly drifted back up onto the side table.

Paul's first urge was to shout for Christy to come back down, but he knew that she would either doubt him or not find the event nearly as magical as he had. He was not enamoured with either option, so he simply sat there by himself, wishing he did not have to call Margaret the following morning.

Switching off the sitting room lights, he headed up to bed. Christy looked to be asleep already, but had left his bedside light on for him. Once he had finished his bathroom routine, he eased himself in beside her. Christy's hand found his under the covers and held it tightly.

"Until I met you that day on the Isle of Wight, I was completely lost."

Paul squeezed her hand.

"From the moment I ran away, I was incomplete. I had no idea who I really was. I didn't know it at the time, but looking back I can see that I was a mess. You changed all that. With you, I found peace and love and most importantly, safety. You wonder why I want this house cleaned immediately? The person responsible for almost destroying me has just died, bringing the first taste of spiritual freedom I've felt since I was a child. I need him to be dead, and to remain dead. I have never believed in an afterlife or spirits that stay behind. I can't, otherwise it opens the door to thoughts of the unspeakable happening. This house cannot have any link to a spiritual reawakening. You understand that, right?"

"Of course, I do," Paul whispered. "I'll call Margaret first thing in the morning."

Christy snuggled into him and Paul turned so that he was facing her. He felt himself growing hard; so did Christy. She flipped over, facing away from him.

"Not until the house is clean," she said.

Paul sighed and rolled away from her.

"I love you," Christy whispered.

"Love you too," he replied.

CHAPTER 18

Margaret answered on the second ring. Paul reckoned that she must have been perched by the phone in the hopes of hearing some gossip from her network of old biddies.

"Paul," she crowed. "How lovely to hear from you. How's Christy and the new house? I was sorry to hear about her father."

Neither of them had spoken to Margaret in months, yet she was as up to date on the status of their lives as they were. They had met Margaret when they had first moved to Twyford and had both started volunteering at a cat sanctuary a few miles out of town. She had been a fellow volunteer, and used to regale them with story after story of cat adoption successes. Their conversations at the cat sanctuary had developed into a loose friendship, and a quarterly lunch at Burrata's restaurant in Ruscombe.

"We're both fine, thank you," Paul replied. "It's funny you should mention the house, that's why I'm calling you."

There was dead silence from the other end.

"Margaret, are you still there?"

"I don't do house cleansing anymore." Her tone had changed dramatically from bubbly busybody to cold neutrality.

"May I ask why?"

There was another lengthy silence.

"I got in a bit over my head," she finally stated. "I was invited to Scotland to cleanse a small bed and breakfast, owned by a friend of a friend, on the south shore of Loch Lochy."

"That sounds rather intriguing," Paul said. "I take it things didn't go well?"

"Let's just say that it wasn't a pleasant entity at all. It was ancient and evil. I was David to the spirit's Goliath, but in my case, I was not the victor. I realised at that point that my abilities were limited to dealing with light-hearted spirits. The darkness that accompanied the entity in Scotland was like nothing I'd ever encountered. It wanted me dead, and I believe if I hadn't dashed off when I did, it would have had its way."

"What if I were tell you that, though we do appear to have a ghost, it seems very benign, even helpful..."

"Then why the need for a cleansing?" Margaret shot back.

Paul explained the situation with Christy and her father's death, trying to keep the specific details of her relationship with the man as vague as possible.

"I thought as much when I first met Christy at the sanctuary. People who have been abused in that manner by a parent have a very diffused aura."

So much for subtlety.

"Would you make an exception in our case, considering the situation with Christy?"

"Describe all your interactions with the entity so far,"

Margaret demanded. "Don't leave out a thing."

Paul told her everything that had happened, right down to Christy's bathroom encounter, the cabinet reshuffle and the wine glass resurrection.

"It does seem to be a pleasant one. It's almost as if it holds no anger against the house or its current occupants. It just seems lost and unable to move to the next plane."

"Does that mean you'll help us?" Paul asked.

"You promise that you're not leaving anything out? I can't walk into another ambush. I'm not strong enough."

"You have my word. Everything we've seen seems to indicate a surprisingly pleasant ghost."

"Entity. We prefer entity. All those dreadful reality television programs which chronicle purported ghost sightings have cheapened the word."

After another brief discussion, Margaret agreed to come by the next morning. It was Christy's first day back at work, so the timing was perfect. Paul felt it best that Christy remained absent for the cleansing. After what she had told him the previous night, he thought it would be easier on her if she came home once the process was complete.

Christy was delighted to hear that Paul had convinced Margaret to come over and cleanse the house the following morning, and she spent the rest of day fiddling in the garden so as not to have to 'share' the inside of her home with the temporary ghostly inhabitant. Paul, because of his work assignment, did not have that luxury, and spent the day writing technical prose on his laptop. Almost as if she had cottoned on to what he and Christy were planning, the ghost did not interact once, and Paul felt mildly put out when he had to open the cutlery drawer by himself.

*

Margaret arrived at exactly nine o'clock, as arranged, alighting from her tiny car holding a floral carpet bag that Paul thought looked scarily like the one Mary Poppins had carried in the original movie. A tall woman in her early sixties, she was dressed in her signature, ankle-length, black pleated skirt and a bright, floral blouse.

Margaret breezed through the house, room by room, ending up in the master bedroom, and promptly announced that the entity did indeed seem benign. She had wanted to go up into the attic, but Maggie refused to be budged from where she was stationed under the hatch.

"It's no bother," Margaret said. "I am feeling her presence perfectly well down here."

"What are you going to do now?" Paul asked. "Do we have enough people for a seance?"

"My dear boy, you really must stop watching trash. A seance is nothing but theatre, structured in such a way as to make the attempted contact with the entity seem successful, even when performed by complete charlatans. All I need is a straight-backed chair and a side table, placed at the strongest point of energy. Your bedroom would seem to fit that bill."

"Nothing else?" Paul asked. "Just a chair and a table?"

"Of course there's more," she said, with a wicked smile. "I'll need a strong cup of tea, milk and two sugars, and a digestive biscuit, if possible."

Paul smiled as he retrieved one of their old dining chairs from the nearest spare room and placed it in the centre of the master bedroom, as instructed. Disappearing into their walk-in wardrobe, he returned with a ratty old side table that Christy had found at a charity shop, and had since been using as a place to dump her clothing accessories. He placed it where Margaret pointed as she began tipping things out of her carpet bag, then went downstairs to make the tea. Walking into the kitchen, he stood by the cutlery drawer, hoping for one last bit of mischief from the ghost before Margaret performed her cleansing.

Nothing happened.

It was obvious to Paul that the spirit was fully aware of what was about to happen; it knew that if Margaret did in fact know what she was doing, she would guide the entity into the light and out of the house forever. Paul poured boiling water over a builder's tea bag, waiting until the water in the mug had darkened to a suitable shade before adding a splash of milk. Grabbing the sugar bowl from the cabinet, he was about to spoon some into the mug when he noticed an upside-down smiley face gazing forlornly back at him from the milky tea. He stared at it with a heavy heart; it was obviously the ghost's way of saying goodbye.

Breaking the melancholy moment, he added two spoonful's of sugar and carried the mug of tea and a couple of biscuits back up to Margaret. She was seated on the provided chair and had surrounded herself with various polished crystals. A single stick of incense was positioned in a silver vase, sending a vertical spiral of lavender infused smoke up to the ceiling. Maggie was sitting a few feet from her, looking both concerned and curious.

Paul placed the tea and biscuits where indicated.

"What else can I do?" he asked.

"If you don't mind, I would like to be left completely on my own for a while," Margaret replied. "I'll let you know when I'm done."

"I'll be working downstairs if you need me. Do you want me to take Maggie downstairs with me? I don't want her in the way."

"No, she's fine where she is. Animals are wonderful receptors for lost entities. She may help guide it to me."

Paul smiled, all the while wondering what he had gotten himself, and now poor Mags, into.

Retreating downstairs, he settled himself at the dining table and continued his writing for Mashihoto's latest gadget.

After a while, he heard Margaret calling to someone in a gentle but firm voice. Her one sided conversation went on for over an hour, until there was suddenly complete silence from upstairs. Just as Paul was in the middle of desperately trying to find the best phrase to describe the high-speed function of the new product he was working on, the entire house shook, causing Paul to almost jump out of his seat in surprise. The shaking only lasted for a second, but it was enough to send all the hanging lights swinging back and forth.

Moments later, he almost jumped again as Margaret let out a piercing scream.

Her cry was followed by the sound of charging feet on the stairs. Maggie bounded into view first, dashing though the sitting room and under Paul's chair, her whole body shaking and her fur standing up so straight that it looked as though it had been glued in place. Margaret swiftly followed, her face white as a sheet, sweat glistening on her face. Her Mary Poppins bag was open, and some of its contents were hanging precariously out of one side. She looked at Paul, and he could see that her eyes were glazed over. It looked as if she had been crying.

"I'm sorry," she babbled. "I don't know what happened." Everything was perfect then... I can't go through this again."

She started for the front door.

"Did you get rid of her?" Paul called after her.

"Yes!" she shouted back, as she reached for the handle.

"Then what's the problem?"

Margaret froze at the door and looked back at him with haunted eyes.

"She wasn't the only one here."

CHAPTER 19

Paul watched Margaret swerve at high speed down the driveway, clipping the hedge at the bottom as she did so, before disappearing down the tiny lane. He was at a compete loss as to what he should do next. He did not know what Margaret had done, or what she thought she had done. He could not even be sure that she had cleared out the ghost. He had always been somewhat doubtful of her mental faculties, not to mention her newfound interest in 'house cleansing'. Unfortunately, there was no way to find out if she was in fact any good at it; the spirits she had supposedly 'led to the other side' were unlikely to return just to give her a reference.

He started to worry about what to tell Christy. Should he tell her what Margaret had said about the possible other entity? Or should he just tell her that Margaret had told him she had removed the ghost, as requested? The second option was at least partially true, and would save Christy worrying. The more he thought about it, the more he liked the second option. If his ghost was still there, hopefully she would stay quiet and not do anything mysterious or magical while Christy was in the house. That way she could stay, and no one would be any the wiser.

Paul was fairly certain that Margaret's words about the 'other entity' were complete nonsense. No doubt she was still shell shocked from whatever had happened in Scotland, if indeed anything had actually happened in Scotland. Paul reasoned that her sanity must be starting to slip, and that she was simply sensing demons where there were none.

Back inside the house, Paul spent a minute trying to determine whether he could sense anything untoward. He had zero knowledge of what 'spiritual energy' was supposed to feel like, but he assumed that something terrifying enough to scare the living daylights out of someone like Margaret must emit some sort of tangible vibe.

He got nothing. The inside of their home felt calm and welcoming. There was nothing out of the ordinary, except that Maggie was still hiding under the chair, cringing as she stared solemnly at the steps leading upstairs. Paul sat and stroked her gently until her ears started to perk up and her fur resumed its usual position.

"It's okay, lovely girl. That silly woman's gone now. Whatever scared you has gone too."

Maggie let out an amazingly long sigh, then rested her head on her front paws.

Paul worked for another hour before making himself a cold tuna salad burrito, a recipe of his own invention, which he ate whilst looking out at the back garden and woods beyond. He hoped that their little start-up problem with the house was fully resolved now, and that they could start finally enjoying the place.

At four o'clock, his alarm went off to remind him to take

another break. Without it, Paul would keep writing until he fell asleep at his screen; the alarm was there to get him away from the laptop for a few minutes, so that he could experience at least a little life through his own eyes. Blinking, he decided that what he and Maggie both needed was a good walk around the property. The clouds were drawing in again, and the light was starting to fade. Better get a walk in now in case it decided to rain later.

Paul smiled down at Maggie.

"Walkies?" Paul asked.

Maggie usually bounced to her feet and knocked over people and furniture in her excitement to get outside, but on this occasion, despite hearing the magic words, she simply sighed again and almost reluctantly got to her feet, meandering half-heartedly towards the back door. Paul watched her with concern. Something must have really spooked the poor animal.

Once outside, Maggie seemed to regain some of her usual boisterous spirit, and they covered most of the land immediately surrounding the property, including the creepy woods along the back. Fortunately, the strange mushroom circle appeared to have lost some of its original eeriness, especially after Maggie decided to piddle on one of the mushroom clusters.

In the western most corner of the plot, they stopped, and Paul looked back at the house with what he hoped was an unbiased appraisal, considering the goings on of the last few days. To his great relief, all he saw was a house. A lovely house, despite the hodgepodge of additions. A single band of sunlight had managed to drill through the grey sky directly behind him, briefly illuminating their home in rays of golden light, before the bullying clouds bunched together, shutting off that day's quota of sunshine.

Maggie had definitely calmed down now that they were away from the house, and Paul became convinced that the old girl had developed some sort of relationship with their wayward spirit, and had been moping ever since Margaret had sent the entity away.

He knew how she felt. Since the ghost had been banished to wherever such spirits ultimately go, he had been feeling rather gloomy himself. Despite having not really had time to grow close to the spirit, they had still developed a sort of daily routine. He would have liked to know more about her, but could not fault Christy for not wanting anything to do with the spirit world at this point in her life. She had enough on her plate without having to deal with her husband having an invisible friend.

Just as they were finishing their wander, Christy pulled up on the driveway, and Maggie charged towards her car, leaping up at her before she had even opened the door.

"You two look like you've had fun day," Christy commented, as she eased herself out of her car and rubbed Maggie behind the ears. "How did things go with Margaret?"

"She was here for just over an hour and as far as I can tell, and the ghost is gone. I had to open the cutlery drawer all by myself..."

"You poor thing," Christy laughed.

"How was your first day back?" Paul asked, hoping to change the subject.

"Busy. Remember when I told you that they said not to worry about anything and that they had my back?"

"I do," he said, knowing that her story was not going to end well.

"Other than a few priority clients with deadlines and court dates, they basically did nothing. I had over a thousand unanswered emails in my inbox, and none of my briefs have been reviewed or acted upon. It's a nightmare."

Maggie, as if sensing that Christy was in a bad mood, leaned all her weight on Christy's thigh, trying to get as close to her as possible.

"Is it too early for a drink?" Christy asked.

"Not for an alcoholic," he replied.

"Phew. That's a relief," she grinned. "I'll have a G and T, please."

"Single or double?"

Her glare answered his question.

As Paul made for the kitchen, Christy headed upstairs to rid herself of her business attire. Maggie started to follow her, but once she saw that Christy was heading for the master bedroom, she stopped at the far end of the hallway, looking on with sad eyes as she lowered herself to the floor.

"Paul?" Christy shouted from upstairs.

He cringed, wondering what she had seen.

"I'm making your drink," he replied.

"Would you come up here, please?" It was clear from her tone that it was not really a question.

"Please don't have found a ghost. Please don't have found a ghost," Paul whispered to himself as he cautiously climbed the stairs.

When he walked into the bedroom, he instantly knew what had pissed Christy off, and he felt himself sigh with relief, despite Christy's irritated expression. For once, the issue did not relate to a ghostly presence, but instead related to the detritus left behind by the ghost cleanser. Paul had completely forgotten to check the bedroom after Margaret had fled from the house earlier that day, though given the speed of her departure, he should have anticipated that the room would be in a bit of a state.

The dining chair and the side table were still where Paul had placed them, but scattered haphazardly around the rest of the room were a bizarre collection of items that must have spilled from her bag. Crystals, smudge sticks and incense were interspersed amongst personal items, including two scarves, a mascara applicator, lipstick and a pack of unopened face masks. There was also what appeared to be the remains of a squashed digestive biscuit.

"Wow... looks like she had quite the party."

"What was she doing up here?" Christy asked.

"This is where she wanted to work. She said something about feeling the spirit more strongly in this room."

"Did you see what she actually did?"

Paul shook his head.

"Other than giving her a chair, a table and a cup of tea, I left her to get on with it."

"I think you forgot the digestive," Christy added, as she prodded a larger piece of the decimated biscuit with her shoe. "You didn't hear anything strange going on while she was here?"

"Of course I did. She's a daft old psychic. She babbled on

up here for over an hour. I couldn't make out what she was saying, but from the bits I could hear it sounded like a one-sided conversation."

"So, she was talking to someone?" Christy asked.

"I didn't say that. I said she was having a one-way conversation. As far as we know, she might do that all day long. The big question is whether anything or anyone ever answers her."

"How did she seem when she left?" Christy asked.

This was the part he had been dreading. He hated lying to Christy, and avoided doing so unless absolutely necessary; even then, it was usually to save her from worrying.

"She didn't say much," Paul extrapolated. "She just said that the ghost was gone, then she left."

"Leaving this mess? That doesn't sound like her."

To Paul's horror, Christy produced her phone from her jacket pocket.

"Hey Siri... call Margaret Barnett."

"There was something..." Paul started to say.

Lara's Theme from Doctor Zhivago suddenly filled the bedroom, accompanied by a vibrating sound. A spectral grey light illuminated the underside of the bed, casting eerie shadows across a few errant dust bunnies that had formed since the room had last been cleaned.

Christy crouched down and reached under the bed, sliding Margaret's bejewelled phone into view.

She looked confused.

Paul felt relieved.

"How could she have forgotten her phone?" Christy

asked him.

"I'm just the bloke who delivers the tea and biscuits." Paul stated.

"I'm serious. I know she doesn't have a landline, so her mobile's all she's got. She must know where she left it. Why hasn't she come back to pick it up?"

"Why are you asking me? I have no idea why she does what she does. She's a nutter."

"It's just odd... why would she leave her phone under the bed and the room in such a mess? Please tell me you haven't killed her and buried her in the woods," she joked.

Paul laughed a little too quickly.

"The woods! Why would I go all the way out there when we have a perfectly good attic?"

Christy smiled, but unconsciously glanced upwards.

Lara's Theme once again filled the room. Christy put the phone on speaker.

"Hello, Margaret's phone," she answered.

"Thank heavens." Margaret sounded more than a little intoxicated. "I've been looking for the blasted thing all afternoon."

"Well, it's here at the house," Christy told her. "You can pick it up anytime."

There was a long silence.

"Margaret? Did you hear me? You can pick it up anytime."

"I'd rather not," she slurred. "Could you be a dear and drop it off?"

"What do you mean you'd rather not?" Christy asked.

"I'm sorry, but I categorically refuse to have to deal with

that man ever again."

The call ended abruptly.

Christy turned to her husband with a questioning look.

"Don't look at me," he pleaded. "I have no idea what she's on about. You heard her voice. She's completely sozzled."

"You didn't tell her about your views on psychics, did you?"

"Of course not," Paul insisted. "I told you, I got her the table and chair, made her a cup of tea then left her completely by herself."

"Then who the hell is she refusing to deal with?"

"Who knows. The woman is a complete nut job. I have no idea who she's ticked off with, but I give you my word that it's not me."

"I wonder if we should have called in a professional after all?" Christy mused.

"Margaret did say that the ghost was gone, so let's just see what happens, shall we?" Paul suggested.

Christy visibly relaxed, closing her eyes as she stepped into his arms.

"It would be nice if she really has gone. I'd like a little bit of peace in our lives for a change."

Paul kissed her on the nose.

"The house is ours now. We should start to enjoy it."

Unseen by the pair, Maggie suddenly jumped to her feet and lunged at the hallway wall.

CHAPTER 20

While Christy changed, Paul began preparing Spaghetti Bolognese from scratch. It was Christy's favourite dinner, within Paul's limited culinary repertoire, and by the time she came downstairs, looking refreshed and a little more relaxed, the sauce was simmering.

Paul handed her a tall gin and tonic, made with her favourite Hendrick's gin. It was a warm night for late September, so they decided to sit outside and admire the garden as the light slowly faded. The only garden furniture they owned was a pair of horrid white, metal fold-out chairs, as uncomfortable as they were ugly, but since they had not got around to buying anything new, the hideous chairs were their only option.

As it grew dark, a few lights from the village and surrounding properties gave off just enough of a glow for Christy and Paul to make out where their property ended and the next began. At the other end of the garden, no light penetrated beyond the first row of trees; beyond that line, there was nothing but blackness, the shapeless outline of the wood seeming darker that night itself.

"It's been an eventful few months, hasn't it?" Christy sighed.

"Especially for you. How you stayed in that house for all those weeks, I will never know. Weren't you scared?"

"Of what? A helpless old man who didn't have the strength to get out of his wheelchair?" she replied.

"I was thinking more about the memories that being there must have brought back," Paul said.

"That's the funny thing. By going back there, I came to understand that the memories had never left me. They were part of me. They were interlaced with my thoughts, my decisions... everything. By staying there, especially after he died, I honestly believe that I finally came to understand that they were just that: memories. I realised that they weren't tangible; they couldn't hurt me anymore unless I let them."

Christy took a sip from her drink.

"Looking back, I know that, to some extent, I felt guilty for what happened."

"Oh, honey," Paul interrupted. "That's ridiculous. You were a child. There was nothing you could have done."

"Yes, there was," Christy continued. "There was always something I could have done. I could have said something at school. Told a friend. Gone straight to the police."

"Then why didn't you?" Paul asked gently.

"Because I was ashamed. At first, I felt embarrassed that my parents were fighting. Even when he beat her, I didn't want my friends to know that my family was so messed up. When he started on me, I could only imagine what would have happened if other people knew. At least that's the way I thought, back then. I was more worried about people knowing about it and judging me than stopping my father from…"

"I know," Paul said. "And now?"

"Now I know that gossip would have been a far better alternative to the three years of misery I chose to endure."

"You didn't choose anything. In fact, you never had a choice in the matter. He knew that you trusted him; he abused his position to take advantage of you. Every time you think any thoughts about it being your fault, you need to remind yourself that he was the monster. You were just the prey. You must realise just how sick a man has to be for him to do that to his own child. There's no rationale that can excuse his actions."

Christy held her hand out. Paul took it in his.

"It's over now," Paul said. "You're home. You're safe, and you have a wonderful life ahead of you."

"I'm loving you a lot at the moment," she said.

"Me too, you."

As Paul released her hand to grab his drink, a small cloud of midges descended on the pair. Laughing, the couple began to swat at them like crazy, trying to convince the bugs to go elsewhere.

Then the bats came.

Drawn in by the tiny insects, numerous bats began to swoop down into the midge cloud, and within seconds, there were dozens of the shadowy creatures, feasting only inches from their faces. The two of them dropped to the ground to try and avoid the flying rodents, but the midges followed their body heat, and the bats followed the bugs. Finally, after swatting at their attackers for what seemed like an eternity, Christy and Paul managed to crawl through the French doors and scoot inside without letting anything follow them in. Collapsing onto the floor, they realised immediately that they had an entirely new dilemma.

They had left their gin and tonics outside.

Glancing at one another's panicked expressions, they burst out laughing again, and decided that the drinks could wait until the morning. They had almost finished them anyway, so not too much gin had been wasted.

After helping Christy up, Paul went into the kitchen to prepare the pasta, filling their largest pot with water and placing it on the hob to boil. Adding some of the last ingredients to the sauce, he stirred the Bolognese a few times, then turned to check on the water. It was barely moving, let alone boiling. Puzzled, he checked the flame, and was stunned to see that the hob had somehow switched itself off.

Confused, Paul turned the gas back on and continued with the sauce prep, checking the water again after about five minutes. Once again, there was no flame, and the knob had been switched to the off position. Staring at the oven, he felt the beginnings of a chill run up his back.

This time, Paul stood in front of the pot until it started to boil, then threw in the spaghetti, never taking his eyes off flaming hob ring. Christy walked in to grab the table settings, expecting Paul to turn and look at her, but her husband's eyes remained fixed on the hob.

"What are you doing, honey?"

"Making sure the water stays boiling," he replied.

Christy gave him a sideways glance as she gathered the forks and spoons, then walked out of the room, leaving her husband to his eccentric vigil. A few minutes later, the pasta was cooked, and the sauce was ready. Paul turned to grab the colander from an under-counter cabinet, but the cupboard door was already open.

Staring at the open cupboard, Paul had no choice but to accept the possibility that Margaret had failed to rid the house of the ghost. He was going to have to tell Christy... but how? And when?

Walking out of the kitchen, Paul served up the spaghetti and poured them each a glass of Burgundy.

"How can we know for certain that the ghost is really gone?" Christy asked, causing Paul to choke on a mouthful of pasta.

"Margaret said she was, so I guess we have to believe her. She's the closest thing we have to an expert, after all," he managed to say, once he had managed to swallow his mouthful of Bolognese.

"Do you trust her?" she asked.

Paul thought of a hundred different answers, but none of them were helpful in his current situation.

"I don't see that we have a choice," he responded, hoping that she would not see through his fabrication.

"I suppose you're right. You would tell me if you felt anything strange in the house, wouldn't you?"

"As if you need to ask."

"Thank you for making my favourite dinner tonight. Your Bolognese always cheers me up."

After dinner, they snuggled up together on the couch, with Maggie stretched across their laps. After the bat attack, Christy felt it was only fitting to keep the chills going, and she decided they should watch the original version of *The Grudge*, one of the best exports to come out of Japan since sushi and Godzilla.

As was often the case when they watched a movie after a few glasses of wine and a hard day at work, Christy was asleep within the first fifteen minutes, with Paul managing just under an hour before he too drifted off. It was not until the intensity of the music reached a crescendo that he jolted awake, opening his eyes.

Paul watched the screen as the double-jointed corpse of a young girl creaked down the stairs of a contemporary Japanese home. The girl's soaking wet, black hair was plastered against her head, and she was slowly approaching the camera.

Maggie chose that moment to begin whining in her sleep, somehow adding to the horror. Paul knew the scene by heart, but though he wanted to see it through, he felt his eyes starting to close. Then, something changed. There was something wrong with the TV screen. The image was suddenly sharper; more lifelike. It almost had a 3D-like quality to it.

Paul sat bolt upright as a bloodied hand emerged from the television, as if there was no screen to stop it. The rest of the contorted body followed suit, accompanied by a loud croaking and rattling sound. The corpse dropped the final few centimetres to the floor, then stopped. The head rose. Paul could just made out the bluish face behind the hair. Only this time, it was not a young Japanese girl at all. It was him... it was him as an eight-year-old boy.

The rattling sound grew louder as the child rose onto its

arms and legs. Its joints were somehow reversed, giving it a spider-like appearance. Suddenly, it skittered towards him with amazing speed, and when it was less than a metre away, it launched itself at him.

Paul screamed, reflexively closing his eyes before the thing struck.

He felt nothing.

Paul cautiously opened one eye and saw the credits rolling on the TV. Christy was still next to him, but Maggie was gone.

"What's up, honey?" Christy asked sleepily.

"I just had a really creepy nightmare. The girl from the bath came out of the TV, only it wasn't the girl. It was me."

"That should keep any therapist busy for a few visits," she joked.

"It was so real," Paul whispered, still in shock.

"It wasn't real at all. It was just your brain messing with you." She playfully tapped his forehead. "I'm going to bed. Will you lock up?"

Paul switched off the TV and checked the front and back doors, before washing up their wine glasses and putting some fresh water into the pasta pot so it could soak overnight.

As he was about to turn off the last downstairs light, he heard Maggie lapping at her water.

"That's enough tonight, silly girl. There'll be no midnight walkies."

He waited for her to reappear from the utility room, but instead, she emerged from behind the coffee table, licking her lips and looking pleased with herself. Sauntering past him, she bounded up the stairs. Paul walked over to the coffee table and looked down. It was too dark to see much of anything, so he turned on the nearest table lamp. He felt his stomach knot, a chill spreading from the base of his spine to just below his skull.

The floor was soaking wet from the base of the TV stand to just in front of where he had been sitting. He crouched down and felt the liquid. It seemed to be just water, but had a slightly gooey feel. He brought his hand to his nose.

It smelled like death.

Paul gagged and ran for the kitchen; it was closer than the tiny bathroom. He was sure he was going to vomit, but once he was standing with his head in the sink, the sensation passed. He wiped his face with a damp kitchen towel, taking a few strengthening breaths.

Grabbing the entire roll of kitchen towel, he headed back into the sitting room. He wanted to get rid of whatever the hell was on that floor. It had to have come from Maggie; she must have rolled in something. The last thing he wanted was for Christy to think that something unusual had happened. She seemed to be in a better place now, and he wanted her to stay that way.

He was about to step into the sitting room when he heard the same croaky rattle. The noise was directly behind him. He took a deep breath, but his nostrils were once again assaulted by the putrid odour of death. He felt his legs go rubbery, and for a brief second thought he was going to faint, like he was some ingenue in a 50s horror movie.

Something grabbed his ankle.

Paul woke up. *The Grudge* was still playing on the TV; Ms

165

Geller was about to set fire to the house as the demonic creature stalked her. Christy, meanwhile, was sound asleep on the couch, and Maggie was draped limply across her lap, her tail wagging back and forth, slapping Paul's ankle with every swing.

Christy must have sensed her husband's distress.

"You alright?" she asked, in a sleep-soaked voice.

"I just had a weird dream, that's all," he lied.

"If it involved a dead girl with wet black hair, I'm not really surprised."

Christy stretched and gently eased Maggie onto the floor.

"I'm off," Christy announced, as she started for the stairs.

Maggie followed her with a look of adoration on her face. Paul switched everything off, then checked the doors and windows. He could not help but feel a strong sense of déjà vu.

"I'll be up in a minute," Paul called after her.

Paul walked over to the coffee table and looked around its legs to see if there was any water on the floor. It was as dry as bone. He repeated the examination at the base of the TV stand, with the same results.

He was about to walk away when he saw something waft across the LG logo at the base of the TV. It was a single, long strand of black hair. He started to reach for it, but it retracted back into the television. As the last centimetre passed into the polarised screen, Paul distinctly heard that same sinister, creaky rattle.

He stumbled backwards, only just avoiding the coffee

table. Regaining his balance, he headed for the stairs with significantly more urgency than usual. He could not work out what was happening. What he had seen could not be the work of the entity. No. It was more likely to be the result of stress. He had accepted that the weeks leading up to and following the funeral would be undeniably difficult for Christy, but had assumed that he himself would not suffer too greatly. However, on reflection, the combination of Christy's absence, the funeral, the spirit, the cleansing, the bat attack and a heavy dinner might have been too much to sweep under the emotional carpet.

It also dawned on him that watching one of the creepiest horror movies ever made had probably not been the best idea considering all the recent goings on. Despite his belief in his own emotional fortitude, a cremation and a haunting were probably enough of a catalyst to cause a few insignificant hallucinations.

He loved it when he was able to rationalise his way through the oddities in life. It made him feel in control: logic truly was his greatest weapon.

CHAPTER 21

Christy was up before sunrise – she had a conference call with clients at eight o'clock, and wanted to do some last-minute editing beforehand – so Paul was still asleep when she stepped out of the shower. She glanced at the wall-to-wall mirror above the twin bathroom sinks, watching for the familiar fogged circle. Instead, the entire mirror was coated in a thin layer of steam.

She felt relieved, but also just a tad disappointed. Not that she would admit it in a million years, but part of her regretted removing the spirit without attempting to know more about her and her background. Still, she could not blame herself... after all, the entity had chosen an unbelievably bad day to introduce itself.

Paul stirred as Christy's car crunched its way across the gravel drive. Bleary eyed, he checked his phone, amazed at how early it was. He closed his eyes, and was just thinking about rolling over and enjoying another hour's worth of sleep when a single paw landed on his stomach.

He opened one eye and saw Maggie's big, lovely head only a few centimetres from his own.

"I don't suppose you would consider making your own breakfast today, would you?"

Maggie tilted her head, as if contemplating his request. Her single bark was answer enough. Paul swung his feet onto the wooden floor and was immediately reminded of his need for some new slippers. It was freezing, and it was not even October yet. He momentarily regretted not bringing his raggedy old pair from the rental, but Christy had made it clear that she was completely done with seeing him in footwear that should have been binned a decade earlier.

He threw on a pair of New Balance trainers and followed Maggie downstairs to the utility room. Opening her food cupboard, he used a scoop to transfer her breakfast measure of dog biscuits into a stainless steel bowl, jumping backwards in shock as a thumb-sized cockroach fought its way to the top of the dish and scurried under the clothes dryer.

Paul peered inside the twenty kilogram bag, but could not see any others. This was all he needed. If there was one thing that Christy truly hated, it was cockroaches. They had once left a rental less than a week after a single cockroach had run along the rim of the bath while Christy was bathing. It had been happily wandering around the tap end of the tub, seemingly completely unaware of Christy's presence until she had started screaming.

Paul pulled everything out of the utility room storage cupboards; he even managed to move the washer and dryer far enough out from the wall to see underneath them, all to no avail. He could not find the culprit. He knew very well that cockroaches were not solitary creatures; if you saw one, there would be more.

Sometimes many more.

Disheartened, he returned everything to its proper place, ate a quick breakfast, and headed to the local shop on Hurst's picturesque high street. Despite its relatively small size, Paul found that the shop always seemed to have at least one of whatever he needed. On that day, he needed cockroach killer, and they had three of them. He could always order some traps or more spray on Amazon if he needed to.

As he was about to climb into his car, he heard footsteps approaching. Looking up, he saw the weird old man from the pub garden shuffling towards him. In an introverted panic, Paul shut the car door and drove away as fast as he could. He did not have the time or the energy to deal with the old man and his strange stories.

"Shit..."

Paul slammed on his brakes. Perhaps he should have stayed to talk to the old man... his stories might help to explain what the hell was happening back at Croft House. He looked in his rear-view mirror, but could not see the old man anywhere. He had vanished, again.

Once back home, Paul took the three traps to the kitchen and opened one. Having confirmed that they were harmless to pets, Paul opened the other two packs then placed those in the utility room, one under the washer and one under the dryer. The other one went under the sink in the kitchen. Paul planned to check later to see if any bug had wandered in.

After two hours of intense writing and editing, he stopped to stretch and walk in a circle, to keep his limbs from cramping. As he was pacing the downstairs rooms, he heard a scratching sound coming from the kitchen area. He stopped to listen, but realised it was coming from the utility room. He stood still until he heard it again. A smile formed on his face.

He had captured his first victim.

He picked up the box and could hear a cockroach running around inside.

"Sorry, but you started this."

He put the box back under the dryer to let whatever was supposed to happen, happen.

Paul returned to his work, putting in another ninety minutes before he felt the first pangs of hunger for lunch. He raided the fridge for the fixings needed for a sandwich, then laid the items out on the counter in priority order. Opening the cutlery drawer for a knife, he jumped backwards as a cockroach scuttled out and fell to the floor.

Paul watched in amazement as it darted under the kitchen cabinets, through an almost invisible space between two of the adjoining plinths. Paul dropped to his knees and tried to see behind the gap, but he could not get his head close enough to have a serious look. Retrieving a torch and a heavy duty screwdriver from the utility room, he pried off one of the pieces of laminated MDF, shining the light under the cupboard.

He could not see the little bastard anywhere, though he did get a glimpse of the detritus left behind by the kitchen cabinet installer. The beautiful tiled floor ended abruptly just out of view the human eye, with wood shavings, bent screws, broken bits of tile, cigarette butts and even what looked to be the mummified body of a tiny rodent decorating the rest of the netherworld where no person was ever meant to explore.

He got to his feet, and was about to replace the laminate plinth when he saw a flicker of movement in the corner of his eye. Turning his head, he discovered three sizeable cockroaches wandering amongst the items he had set out for his lunch.

"Hey, piss off," he shouted at the trio.

He reached over and tried to stab one of them with his screwdriver, missing the insect and skewering a block of cheddar cheese instead. The cockroaches scattered in different directions, disappearing through minuscule cracks and joins between the countertop and the cabinets at such speed that Paul only managed to follow one of them.

The cockroach in question had somehow managed to squeeze itself between two sections of the granite splashback, where a tiny section of sealant had worn away over time. Digging the screwdriver blade into the gap, Paul forced one of sections away from the wall, breaking the granite strip in the process. Too focussed on the hunt to realise what he had done, Paul continued to wrench the rest of the granite away from the wall, only to discover that the cockroach had mysterious disappeared.

Furious, he crouched down again, trying to figure out how to see behind the lower cabinets, when a shadow passed across the polished stone countertop. Looking up, he saw the clear silhouette of another cockroach within one of the kitchen's domed glass lights, scurrying around the inverted bowl like a skateboarder.

Paul ran into the utility room and retrieved a folding

ladder, positioning it under the light fixture and climbing up with slow, steady movements, hoping to avoid alerting the cockroach to his presence. The rim of the light fitting hung about ten centimetres from the ceiling. Paul's plan was to sweep his hand around the inside of the bowl, forcing the insect onto the floor where it could then be dealt with.

Unfortunately for Paul, the plan did not go well. He managed to reach into the frosted glass dome, but could not manoeuvre his hand around the central support rod. The cockroach, meanwhile, saw his hand as a potential escape route, and promptly shimmied onto his fingers, across his wrist, and under the cuff of his shirt.

Paul screamed and tried to pull his hand free, but his watch caught on the lip of the bowl, causing the whole fixture to tip towards him. At the same time, another cockroach that he had not seen slid along the interior of the glass, straight towards his face. Paul reacted instinctively and recoiled backwards, tipping the ladder onto its side. With no hope of regaining sure footing, he grabbed the light fitting with both hands, and for a brief moment, as he swung above the kitchen floor, he thought that he might have avoided catastrophe.

Then the entire light fitting, and a decent chunk of the ceiling, gave in to gravity.

Paul hit the floor first, the rest of the debris raining down on him a millisecond later, but he had no time to evaluate his condition, for he could feel the first cockroach continuing up his arm, towards his shoulder. In a panic, he ripped his shirt off and threw it as far away he could within the confines of the kitchen. Like a madman, he sat there, covered in plaster dust and lamp parts, wondering what the hell was coming next.

Unbeknownst to Paul, though he had managed to extricate himself from the shirt, the catalyst to the whole debacle was still on his body. The cockroach had reached his neck, and after making the executive decision to travel down rather than up, it decided to nestle itself amidst Paul's chest hair.

Paul's scream must have been audible in the next county, as he tore at his chest, trying to extricate the creature. The cockroach however, realising that it's hiding place was no longer safe, ran south at full tilt. Paul began jumping up and down like he was walking over hot coals, slapping at his stomach and managing to whack himself firmly in the balls, unable to tell whether the cockroach had been knocked free or not.

Taking a moment to breathe, he stood stock still and surveyed the floor and himself. He felt sure that his trouser belt was cinched tightly enough to negate the likelihood of the insect having passed any lower, but just to be sure, he set every nerve ending below his waist to high alert. Then, stretching over to the nearest drawer, he opened it, with the intent of grabbing the fly swatter within.

The second he opened the drawer another cockroach poked its head out. Its antennae were whipping about in all directions, checking for something. Seemingly satisfied, it climbed out, followed by a dozen others. Paul instantly forgot about the one he had been hunting and tried to slam the drawer closed on the larger gathering, but as his hand touched the laminate, the drawer flew out of its slot and thousands of cockroaches erupted from the opening like a black surge of projectile vomit.

Paul could not move. It was like he was stuck in one of the dreams he had experienced as a child when confronted with terror. He was frozen in place. As he watched, a second drawer, then a third, flew open, followed by cascading waterfalls of insect invaders. The kitchen floor was starting to fill with their wiggling, crawling bodies, and their hard, flexible plates clacked against one another, making a sound like Rice Krispies amplified through a speaker system.

The walls of the kitchen turned black as still more insects streamed down from the ceiling, and within seconds, every cabinet and appliance was gushing with black cockroaches. In frozen disbelief, Paul watched in horror as they began to crawl up the inside of his trouser legs.

*

Frank Helms was driving his Thames Water van up the narrow lane to Croft House. It had been a long day already, and it was only just past one o'clock. He sighed. The normally courteous greeting he received from homeowners when he stopped to read their water meters had been drastically modified since COVID. He now had to practically beg to be allowed entry, and even then, he had to mask and glove up with fresh kit each time he entered somewhere new. He wondered what the reaction would be from the owners of Croft House.

Killing the engine, he was about to step out of the van when the front door of the house flew open, and a man in his forties came charging outside. To Frank's surprise, the man was completely naked, save for a pair of colourful socks, and was totally oblivious to Frank and his van. Instead of greeting him, the man ran across the driveway, stopped on the front lawn, then threw himself to the ground and began rolling himself backwards and forwards, screaming 'get off me, get the hell off me!'.

Frank wanted to help, but what with distancing, the man's undeniable nudity, and the fact that he appeared to be completely bonkers, he was not sure what he could really do. Eventually, the poor man managed to get back on his feet, still slapping himself repeatedly all over. Greatly perturbed by his next client's bizarre behaviour, Frank leaned back into the van and pressed his palm against the horn button.

For a small van, it had a big horn, and Frank kept his hand on it until the man snapped out of his delirium and looked over towards the source of the din. Frank doubted he would ever forget the poor man's expression: a mix of shock, fear, realisation and embarrassment.

Paul, after noticing the stranger on his driveway, who appeared to be staring back at him in horrified confusion, slowly forced himself to return to reality. He had no idea what he was doing outside the house, or how he had got there. His mind was too hazy. Trying to drag himself back to the present, he placed his palms gently on his arms and shoulders. Surprised by the feel of skin on skin, he looked down, and quickly realised that he was stark naked. Embarrassed, he tried to cover himself with his hands as he sprinted back towards the house.

"Sorry if this is a bad time, but I need to read your water meter," Frank called after him.

"Hang on a sec," Paul shouted. "I'll be right back."

Paul had no intention of going anywhere near the kitchen, so he ran straight up to his bedroom and threw on a dressing gown, before hurrying back downstairs and poking his head out of the front door.

"Sorry about that," Paul offered.

He desperately wanted to add an excuse, but realised that there was nothing he could say that would not make matters worse or make him appear even more insane, so he decided that the best course of action was to say no more about it.

Frank donned a fresh mask, disposable gloves and shoe covers.

"I have no idea where the meter is," Paul confessed in a shaky voice, as he grabbed his own mask from the table by the front door. "We just moved in."

"It's in a cabinet in the kitchen," Frank assured him. "I've been coming to this house for quite a few years."

Paul felt whatever colour he had left in his cheeks drain away. He could not let the man go anywhere near that room. He did not even know who to call about an infestation of that magnitude. Certainly it was far beyond the capabilities of any spray or cockroach trap. Then there was the damage to the walls and ceiling… Christy was going to give him both barrels when she got home.

Unaware of Paul's inner turmoil, Frank steered around him and walked towards the back of the house. Paul cringed, waiting for a scream.

"Oh," Frank uttered.

"I know. All I did was…"

"You should have said you were in the middle of fixing your lunch," Frank said apologetically. "I could have come back a bit later."

Paul slowly walked into the kitchen, terrified that some new horror would be waiting for him, but as he stepped around the corner, all he would see was Frank, sitting on his knees in front of a low cabinet at the other end of the room.

"I've always liked this house," Frank said. "It's got a happy feel about it. I see more homes than I care to remember; some of them just have a nasty feeling the second you walk in, but not yours."

Paul surveyed the kitchen in wonder. Everything looked exactly as it had before his cockroach encounter. The only things out of place were his sandwich fillings, which were still sitting on the countertop waiting to be converted into lunch, and the cutlery drawer, which was open once again.

Frank got to his feet and stepped around Paul, who was now staring open-mouthed towards far end of the room.

"Right," Frank said. "I'm done. I hope you enjoy the house."

Paul snapped out of his stupor.

"Thank you. I'm sorry about the... the um..." Paul gestured with his head towards to front of the house.

"I didn't see a thing, sir," Frank replied.

It was hard to tell, what with him wearing a mask and all, but Paul was fairly sure that the man had smiled at him.

Paul stood at the front door and watched as the van turned out of sight at the bottom of their drive. He took a deep, strengthening breath, then marched back into the kitchen. The drawer was still open. He stood next to it,

178

waiting for something else to happen. Nothing. Finally, he closed it, turning to the other counter to put his lunch options back in the fridge. Just the sight of the cheese and the packaged ham slices made him feel sick. Food was definitely out of the question.

As he shut the fridge door, he heard a sound behind him, and he spun around, just in time to witness the cutlery drawer opening. Stepping over to it, he reached inside to replace the unused lunch knife, howling in pain as it slammed closed with his fingers still in it.

"Why are you doing this?" he screamed at the ceiling. "I thought we were friends?"

CHAPTER 22

Instead of working on his new manual, Paul spent the afternoon browsing the internet, looking up hallucinations, sleep-state disassociations, and the early signs of delusional insanity. Between *The Grudge* episode and the attack of the cockroaches, he was worried that he was having some sort of mental breakdown.

The reading taught him a lot about how a person could unknowingly fall into a hypnagogic state, dreaming with such reality that it seemed like a hallucination. He read case after case about people who had experienced the most bizarre dreams while being certain that they had at no time been asleep. Some people woke up outside, or in a different house, and in one case, a woman had found herself in a different town.

Some of the instances were linked to the use of sleep medication or the overuse of benzodiazepines, but many were also associated with severe stress. After three hours of research, Paul decided that he did not need to be institutionalised, he simply needed to de-stress. He was relieved, but also frustrated; he had considered himself to be the kind of person who had control over their own mind when it came to dreams and hallucinations. Apparently not.

Paul used the downstairs loo to splash his face with cold water hoping to calm himself down, but when he caught his reflection in the mirror, he could not help but stare at the man in front of him. He looked awful. The dark bags under his eyes came halfway down his face, his pupils were dilated, and his skin seemed to have aged at least ten years.

Breathing on the mirror, he drew a circle in the condensation. Nothing happened. Holding up a finger, he drew two eyes. Still nothing happened. Shrugging, Paul reached out to draw a smiling mouth.

His hand passed straight through the glass.

Panicking, he tried to pull it back when he felt a sharp pain in his wrist. Paul wrenched his hand back out of the mirror. His wrist was bleeding. Frantically, he washed the blood away, revealing the shape of a large bite mark. He looked up at the mirror, just as a smile was drawn onto the fogged glass.

Paul backed out of the tiny room, about to have a full-on meltdown, when it dawned on him that the pain had subsided. He looked at his hand. The mark and the blood were no longer there. Confused, he glanced back at the mirror. All he could see was the condensation, and his half-finished smiley face. Shaken, he went back to the dining table and forced himself to set aside his paranoia, deciding instead to answer the hundred or so emails he had been avoiding.

When Paul's four o'clock alarm went off, he closed the laptop for the day, relieved that Christy would soon be home. He called for Maggie, but there was no response, so he called her name again. Reluctantly, she appeared from behind the door that led to the stairs, her tail down and her eyes melancholy. She refused to meet Paul's gaze.

It was Maggie speak for: 'I may have had a small accident'.

Paul headed upstairs, and was only halfway down the hall when he was hit by the smell of the aforementioned transgression. Tracing the odour to the master bedroom, he followed his nose into the walk-in wardrobe, discovering a fresh twirl of canine poo in the centre of the carpet. The stench was almost overpowering. Sighing, Paul grabbed a handful of loo roll and managed to lift most of the odoriferous pile in one scoop, removing it from the vicinity.

It took almost half an hour of scrubbing to fully remove the mark and the smell, at least on the carpet; despite Paul's rigorous cleaning, the fragrance of fresh shit still lingered throughout the top floor of the house. Paul opened every window in every room, hoping that there would be enough of a draft to cleanse the air, and in one final act of desperation, he spritzed each room with his aftershave.

Christy walked through the front door just as Paul was binning the last of the evidence.

"What's wrong with Maggie? She looks guilty," Christy called from the entry hall.

"No idea..." Paul replied, lying through his teeth.

As Christy walked into the sitting room, she suddenly pulled a face. Paul knew he had been caught.

"The house stinks of cologne. Did you bathe in it?"

She gave him a quick peck on the cheek.

"That's funny," she commented. "The only thing that doesn't smell of aftershave is you. What are you hiding?"

Paul did not even know why he had bothered with the subterfuge. She found him out every time. Hanging his head, he explained that Maggie had left them a small 'gift' upstairs.

"Maybe you didn't walk her for long enough this morning?" Christy suggested.

Paul had known all along that the blame would end up being his to bear. Sighing internally, he escorted Christy to the walk-in wardrobe, and showed her where the incident had taken place.

"I would never have known," she said with a beaming smile. "If you're planning a career as a master criminal, you just need to use less aftershave."

"Duly noted," he nodded.

"I don't want to seem like I'm nagging you, but did you walk Maggie this evening?"

He stared dumbly back at her.

"I felt she had produced enough," he replied feebly.

"I think it's still worth taking her out, just in case."

Paul sighed and went looking for Maggie He found her in the sitting room, huddled against one of the walls. As Paul approached and reached down to stroke her, she flinched.

"What was that for, sweet girl?"

Maggie looked up at him with her big brown eyes.

"Wanna go for a walk?"

Judging by the way she jumped to her feet and danced in a circle, she did.

*

It was Christy's turn to prepare dinner, and that night, they were having salmon steaks and asparagus. Paul kept her

183

company in the kitchen as they shared their days with each other. Christy told him she had a new client, a man who was being evicted from his flat after being laid off during lockdown. The landlord had done the same to a number of residents in his building, and when Christy had visited the block of flats, she had found the place to be neglected, filthy, and in some places downright dangerous.

Christy had duly written a blistering email to the landlord, quoting relevant sections of the Law, including those that had been created to protect renters from unscrupulous landlords during the COVID crisis. She also added that she might have to involve the local council, who would doubtless keep him embroiled in red tape for many years hence. She told Paul gleefully that she had received a one line email from the landlord just before she had left work for the day, which read: 'Past due rents forgiven. Next rent due in three months'.

She could not have anticipated a better end to the day.

When asked how his day had gone, Paul simply shrugged. He had no intention of telling her about the cockroach debacle.

"Just the usual," Paul replied. "At least until Mags decided to leave me that little gift."

"Don't you think it's a little strange for her to have done that in the wardrobe? She doesn't usually have that sort of accident, and the few times we've found a surprise, they've usually turned out to have been cling-ons. From what you described, it sounded sizeable and intentional."

"Do you think she's anxious about something?" Paul asked. "She had that little accident at the rental the day we viewed this house with the estate agent."

"Moves are supposed to be a big contributor to an animal's stress levels," Christy mused. "She has seemed a little odd since we moved in. She was hanging around under that hatch for days, then this. I hope she's all right."

"Well, I can tell you one thing for certain. She hasn't lost her appetite, and her bowels are working perfectly well."

Christy laughed as she was sipping her wine; it almost went up her nose.

"I know I don't always show it, but I do appreciate the way you take care of things around the house," she said, after recovering. "I know how strange it must be for you while I'm away and you're stuck here all by yourself.

"I stay busy. My work projects fill my time well, and once I finish the one I'm working on at the moment, I plan to start tackling our list of household repairs. There's hardly a door that shuts properly."

"It's old. There's always going to be little fixes that need sorting. Just promise me you won't do anything on a ladder unless I'm here to help. I know how clumsy you can be."

Paul's mind flashed back to his vision of clinging to the kitchen light as the ladder fell away.

"Honey, you just went pale," Christy commented, concerned.

"Did I?" he replied casually. "I don't know why. Probably just hunger."

"I'll start dinner in a minute," she said. "You did eat lunch, I hope?"

"I was going to, then changed my mind."

"Paul, you must eat lunch. I know you get carried away

with writing sometimes but it's not healthy to just skip an entire meal."

"Thanks, mum," Paul joked.

"It's your fault for forcing me to act like one," she volleyed back, as she headed into the kitchen to start preparing dinner.

Paul was about to turn on the news when he thought he heard a window bang shut at the front of the house. He could not remember leaving any open, except the ones upstairs when he had been trying to air out the smell of Maggie's little surprise. Walking into the front room, he listened intently. The sound came again. It seemed to be coming from the front sitting room. He walked in, but saw that both leaded windows were firmly closed.

He looked around the room and felt the same comforting warmth as he had when they had first viewed the house. It was not a big room, but there was something incredibly cosy about it. It was part of the original house, and Paul could only imagine the lives that had been lived in that room. When the place had been built, four hundred years earlier, it would have almost certainly been the main room of the house. The quaint open fireplace would have been where the family gathered for light, food and warmth.

They had not done anything with the space yet; there was still no furniture, and only one painting hung on the wall above the roughly-hewn mantlepiece. That picture was the only thing that Christy had taken away from the Southampton house. It was a copy of a lesser known Van Gogh painting, featuring a field of sunflowers stretching out into the distance. The yellows of the flora against the rich cobalt blue of the Mediterranean sky gave the flowers an almost three-dimensional appearance. It had been Christy's mother's favourite picture.

Paul stood in front of the work of art and stared at it. He could not decide if he liked it or not. There was no doubt that it was a Van Gogh, at least a copy of one. His style was unmistakable. It was the subject matter that bothered Paul for some reason. A painting of a vase of sunflowers was fine, but thousands of the plants, caught in mid-undulation by the artist's brush, was a little too much. The sheer volume of flora was almost claustrophobic. Paul also noticed for the first time that, unlike the artist's most famous work, these sunflowers were not particularly healthy looking. Their stalks were overly long, as if the flowers had been left, forgotten in the field, and the flowers themselves had started to droop, their dark centres missing seeds.

Paul was becoming disorientated. He could not remember seeing so much sadness and despair in the painting before. The more he looked, the more depressing he found the piece. It did not show the raw beauty of Provence, instead, it projected neglect; even death. Paul then knew that the flowers were just that. Dead. The farmer had left them to rot under the southern sun. Their stalks had gone brittle. The yellow feathered blooms surrounding the seed pods were not yellow at all; they had been bleached white by the interminable heat. He could even see tiny beetles feasting on the decaying leaves.

Paul started to feel nauseous, and was about to turn away when he noticed something else in the painting. The farthest row of dying flowers was moving. It was hard to make it out, but there was no doubt in his mind that there was motion between some of the rows. Paul shook his head to clear the image, but it was still there. Whatever was causing the flowers to sway and separate was moving to the front of the picture. Paul wanted to turn away, but he could not leave. His mind needed to understand what his eyes were seeing. The thing was getting closer, and it seemed to be gaining speed, cutting through the plants as it came forwards.

Paul could not see what it was, but he got the impression that it was something dark; something without colour or life; something that had never lived. He felt beads of sweat forming on his brow, and his body began to shake from the cold. As if night was falling on the field, the entire picture began to darken, yet even amidst the darkening canvas, whatever was approaching was darker than dark. It was now only a few rows from the front. Paul involuntarily stepped back.

"Ouch," Christy cried. "That was my foot."

Paul turned and saw her grinning back at him.

"I still don't know if I like it or not," she said.

Paul looked back at the painting. Daylight had returned to the canvas. The flowers were healthy; their colours, joyous against the azure sky and warming spring sunshine.

CHAPTER 23

Paul hardly spoke during dinner.

Christy tried throwing out a couple of topics that usually got a rise out of him, but none seemed to work. Eventually, fed up with his silence, she put down her knife and fork and turned to face him.

"What's going on? You haven't said a word since we sat down."

Paul just shrugged. He did not want to tell her about the painting, as it would doubtless lead on to the cockroaches and the mirror incident.

"I can sense when something's wrong. What is it?"

Paul could tell by her expression that she had switched to solicitor mode, which meant she was going to get the truth out of him, no matter what.

Paul downed his glass of wine and took a steadying breath.

"I seem to be having hallucinations," Paul announced.

"What sort of hallucinations? You've always been something of a daydreamer."

"These aren't daydreams," he replied. "These are full blown nightmares, but I'm not asleep."

"That's ridiculous," she insisted. "If your dreaming,

189

you're asleep."

"That's the problem," he insisted. "I'm not asleep."

"Okay. Give me an example."

"Can you try and be a little less of a solicitor about this?" Paul pleaded. "I'm actually rather terrified about the whole thing."

"Oh, honey, I'm sorry. I was just trying to get you to open up." Christy never seemed to realise when she had switched into her solicitor mode. "Can you tell me about one of your hallucinations?" she asked.

"The last one was right before dinner. It happened in the sitting room."

"When I came in and made you jump?"

"Actually, you coming in seemed to stop it. I went into the room because I heard a window slamming shut, but when I got there, they were all closed. For some reason, I turned to look at that painting, but then I started to see things..."

"What sort of things?"

"The flowers were all dead. The whole picture went dark, as if it were night-time."

"Surely that's just your imagination?" Christy suggested.

"Then I saw that something was moving within the painting. It was in the rows of flowers, at the very back of the field, then it started to move towards the front. Towards me. Whatever it was, it was practically at the end of the field when you made me jump. I could almost make out what it was."

"What was it?"

"It was evil," Paul stated.

"I'm sure it was, but what was it? An animal, or…"

"No." Paul interrupted. "It wasn't anything of this earth. It was pure evil."

Christy stared at him with concern.

"What about the other times?"

Paul told her all about the mirror, as well as his battle with the cockroaches. She listened patiently, nodding solemnly as he described the dreams.

"I wasn't going to say anything, but I had rather a horrible dream last night as well." Christy said.

"Want to share?"

She gave him a quick nod before starting.

"I was working in our front garden, but it was different than now. There was no lawn, just flower beds and evergreens. I somehow knew that I wasn't seeing the world through my eyes. I remember feeling happy, and strangely content, when I heard hooves nearing the property. I saw a man climb down from a wooden cart, which was being pulled by two scrawny Shire horses. There were four other men in the cart, but none of them looked towards the house as they continued on their way. The man was older than me, and seemed angry. I somehow knew that he was my husband. I waved and got to my feet. He seemed to not even notice my gesture. Instead, he walked directly towards me, and as he neared, I could see the fury behind his eyes. Then, before I could say anything, he slapped me, knocking me to the ground.

'I have to learn through my brick mason that you've been lying with his apprentice. A mere boy?' the man screamed at me.

'Sir, I know not of what you speak,' I pleaded. 'I spend my day making the house desirable for your return from the mill.'

He then dragged me to my feet and shoved me towards the front door of the house.

'Get inside you ungrateful, lying whore. I'll show you how I deal with traitors,' he fumed.

I stopped and turned to try and explain, but he hit me in the face. It wasn't a slap. It was a full-on punch."

Paul stared at her in shock.

"That's when I woke up," Christy said. "It was horrible. It felt so real."

"It wasn't though, was it? It was just a terrible dream."

"I assumed it was a dream, but you know me. I always need to know more. So, when I got to work, I did a little research on the house."

Christy retrieved her laptop from the coffee table and logged on to the solicitor's-only property registry site, where she had been looking up the ownership history of Croft House. She showed Paul some of the newer registration documents, and some of the older ones. The further back she scrolled, the more discoloured and faded they became. By the 1800s, they were in very bad shape. Christy explained that, back then, houses tended to be bought for life. It was rare for a family to move once they were settled.

The first ownership registration document was dated to 1873, ten years after the Registry Act. The next change of ownership was forty years later. Christy had to enlarge the screen as well as kick up the brightness in order for Paul to read the handwritten scrawl. The first paragraph was all just legalese about the document itself, but the second paragraph was where Christy wanted Paul to start reading. She had even highlighted the important part.

William Dunstable of Tumbold House, Oxfordshire, a professor and a man of letters, will hitherto be referred to as the buyer. The Right Honourable Peter Frake, acting on behalf of Geoffrey Barnes, the late manager of the Twyford Silk Mill, now deceased, will hitherto be referred to as the seller.

"Late?" Paul asked.

"This sale must have happened after his death," Christy concluded.

"Where's the record of him buying the house?"

"There isn't one. Before the Registry Act of 1863, transactions didn't have to be recorded. The participants would personally hold onto whatever documents existed, and sadly, few remain today. I did a couple of other searches which I think you are going to like."

She opened a saved website, showing records of births, deaths and marriages. Her first search had been for Geoffrey Barnes, and she had found something almost immediately. It stated that had died of heart failure in 1872, at the age of forty-seven.

"So, he died eleven months prior to the sale of the house," Paul observed.

Christy nodded, then showed him her search for marriages under the same name. There was a record of marriage, dated eight years prior, between Geoffrey Barnes and Emma Stiles. The recorded address was Croft House.

"Wow," Paul exclaimed. "Nice job. You should do this professionally."

"I do, you prat!" she jokingly shot back.

"Just out of curiosity, did you look for a death record for Emma?"

Christy gave him an 'as if you had to ask' look.

"There is no record of her death. I searched up until the turn of the century."

"Isn't that a little odd?"

"Yes," she stated. "Governmental record-keeping back then was a disgrace, but the local churches were fanatical about recording births and deaths. Their figures were also used whenever a census was carried out."

"So, what happened to her?" Paul asked.

"If there's anything real about my dream, I have a feeling she may have never left the house again after Geoffrey was finished with her."

"You think he kept her prisoner in here?" Paul sounded horrified.

"I don't know, but if he did, I just hope she wasn't still locked up somewhere when he dropped dead."

"Creepy thought," Paul observed. "Are you concerned about any of this?"

"I'm a solicitor. I'm always concerned when I don't have all the facts. However, there's no point worrying too much about something that could be completely unrelated to anything."

To Paul, her open bluntness made her seem even more adorable than normal.

"Don't give me those big lovey eyes of yours," she said, grinning. "We're not christening the bedroom until I am certain that we are completely ghost free."

Sighing dramatically, prompting a laugh from Christy, Paul tidied up the glasses and added them to the washing up pile from dinner, while Christy headed upstairs to carry out her pre-bed bathroom routine. After brushing her teeth and hair, she stopped and looked closely at the mirror. Turning on the hot tap next to the sink, she watched as the steam began to fog the mirror. Once most of the glass had been covered, she drew a circle and two dots, then stood back, waiting for the smile to be created.

"Emma, if you are here, please let us know. We want to help you."

Nothing happened.

She continued to wait until the condensation was almost gone, then wiped the remainder away with a towel and left the room.

*

Paul spent the next day finishing his latest manual, and just a few minutes before three p.m., he typed the last few words and closed his laptop. He knew Tokyo would love the new instructions, and took a moment to bask in the glow of his own achievement, before he was interrupted by Maggie barking furiously somewhere upstairs.

Perturbed by the distress in her tone, he made his way upstairs, and found her in the walk-in wardrobe. She was standing next to a wet spot in the carpet, looking frantic and distressed.

"Maggie?" Paul used his gentle but firm 'what happened' voice.

She looked up at him with confused, sad eyes.

"Let's get you outside in case there's any more in there."

Maggie followed him downstairs, but even once her lead was attached, she seemed unexcited by the prospect of a walk. Concerned, Paul took her along the entire circumference of the property, with the exception of the part at the end of the woods.

Once back in the house, he gathered some kitchen towel and carpet cleaner, managing to blot up most of Maggie's urine before it could soak too deeply into the carpet. As he was about to apply the cleaning spray, he felt the room grow colder. He stood, but could not see the cause.

Now on his feet, he noticed that he was in the perfect spot between the two opposing mirrors to see the infinity reflection effect, and could not resist adjusting his pose and watching the hundreds of reflected Pauls follow suit.

He was just wondering if there was any way to get a photo of the reflection without the phone being visible in the shot when he thought he saw movement in the farthest visible mirror. As he stared down the near infinite line of reflections, he caught sight of it again. It was ridiculously far away, and almost too small to make out; just a tiny dark smudge on the furthest visible reflection.

He was about to turn away when it moved again, somehow shifting from the furthest mirror in the infinity effect to the one before it. Paul stared, but the smudge remained completely still. He realised that though he could see the dark blur on the lower part of the distant mirrors, it was somehow not reflected onto any of the closer ones.

It moved again. This time Paul saw it clearly as it flitted from one mirror to the next, seeming to vanish for a millisecond in between. Just as Paul started doubting his own vision, it reappeared, sliding to the next closest mirror.

It then began speeding up.

Its movement was almost that of an animal jumping from one rock to another, yet its form remained fluid and indistinct. Paul realised then that the temperature in the wardrobe had dropped further still, and goosebumps had appeared on his bare arms. The thing in the mirror had stopped again. It almost looked like a small black cloud, pulsating menacingly as it decided on its next move.

Something made Paul turn and face the opposing mirror, expecting to see the same image, but the black form was not there. Spinning back around, he realised that not only was the dark smudge still there, but it was also much closer, and was now moving rapidly between the reflective surfaces. It was only about twenty mirrors away, and was still speeding up.

Only at that moment did Paul realise that what he was seeing seemed to be after him, but as he tried to step out from between the facing mirrors, the black form reached its final destination.

He was too late.

Unable to move, Paul watched in horror as the dark, swirling mass began to expand, filling the reflective rectangle as it surged with a regular and constant rhythm.

Just before it made one final leap at him, Paul realised that its pulsing was audible. The sound was steady; strong; growing louder every millisecond.

It sounded almost like... a heartbeat.

CHAPTER 24

"Honey?" Christy shouted, as she ran into the house. "I've been trying to call you from the car."

There was no reply. She hung her coat with the others and called Paul again. He did not reply. Instead, Maggie walked in from the sitting room. Christy could tell instantly that there was something wrong with her. Her ears were flat against her head and her tail was tucked tightly between her back legs.

"What's up, Mags?" she asked, stroking the Labrador's forehead. Maggie turned and led Christy to the stairs.

"Paul? Where are you?"

She followed Maggie up the stairs, her internal organs tying themselves in knots. Something was clearly wrong, but she had no idea what.

Maggie led her through to the master bedroom, then into the wardrobe. Paul was lying on his back, apparently fast asleep. Christy shook him but he would not wake up. Panicking, she ran to the bathroom and filled a glass with ice cold water. She tried flicking some onto his face, but there was no response from Paul. Desperate, she emptied the whole glass onto him.

His eyes opened in shock as he choked on the water.

"What the hell?" he stammered.

"What the hell to you too," Christy exclaimed. "You scared the bejesus out of me. What do you think you're doing, passed out in the wardrobe?"

Paul sat up and took in his surroundings.

"I have no idea. I remember cleaning up some piss that Maggie left for me... then nothing. What time is it?"

"It's just turned six," she replied.

"Six? I came up at four..." he stated, in a worried tone. "I wonder if there was something in the cleaning fluid I used on the carpet."

"I doubt it. Besides, I don't smell a thing in here. Are you sure you even cleaned the carpet? The bottle still has its plastic tab set to 'off'."

Paul tried to put the pieces together, but his mind was a complete fog. He could remember everything that had happened before the blackout, but nothing after.

"Let's get you downstairs," Christy suggested.

Paul obediently followed her out of the bedroom, but Maggie stayed behind, staring into the darkness.

She began to growl.

*

Christy settled Paul at the dining table, then went to get him a glass of water, grabbing a clean tea towel from the drawer so he could mop off the remains of the liquid she had tipped over his head.

"Do you feel dizzy or faint?" she asked.

"No. Just really tired. I could sleep for days."

"Are you having problems with your writing? I know you get a bit off when you are."

"No," he answered. "In fact, I finished the last draft for this product today."

"Maybe that's it," Christy suggested. "It's obviously been a difficult one, maybe finishing it triggered some sort of mental release."

"I don't know. I just want to go to sleep."

"Do you think you can manage to stay awake while I cook some pasta? We can throw in some of that Waitrose fresh pesto you like. Maybe a glass of Sauvignon will perk you up?"

"I'm willing to try," he smiled up at her.

As she put a pot of water on to boil, she called out to him from the kitchen.

"Do you want penne or tagliatelle?"

Paul stared blankly, straight ahead.

"Honey, did you hear me?" Christy shouted from the other room.

Paul's head suddenly rocked backwards, such that his face was pointing towards the ceiling.

His jaw flew open.

At first, only a tiny wisp of black, cloud-like vapor rose from his mouth and nose. Then, in one expulsive burst, a plume of inky black smoke exited Paul's body and quickly dispersed within the air. As it passed through the overhead chandelier, the crystal light fitting rocked back and forth, its candle shaped bulbs flickering on and off.

Christy walked into the room and was shocked to see her husband sitting there with his head at such a severe angle.

"Honey... Paul?" she asked, as she approached him.

His head slowly tipped forwards and he let out a huge

yawn.

"What just happened?" he asked.

"That's what I want to know," Christy stated. "It looks like you just passed out again."

"That's odd. I feel great. What's for dinner?"

Despite his sudden return to normality, Christy was not buying it. She took his temperature and activated his smart watch, checking his pulse, blood pressure and blood oxygen levels. All were within normal range.

"You know what I fancy," Paul mused. "A nice glass of Sauvignon and some penne with fresh pesto."

"Are you having a laugh?" Christy asked.

Paul looked at her with complete confusion.

"No, I just suddenly fancy some vino and pasta."

With her eyebrows furrowed, she went back into the kitchen to add the penne to the water.

Over dinner, Paul seemed to have returned to his normal self. The feeling of exhaustion had vanished.

"I forgot to tell you, I saw that old man from the pub garden yesterday."

"What did he have to say?" she asked.

"Not much. I drove away before he could say much of anything," Paul admitted.

"How mature of you," she said, shaking her head.

"I changed my mind halfway up the road and stopped the car, but he had already vanished."

"He seems to be very good at that," she commented. "He must be faster than he looks."

"Or perhaps he's another ghost," Paul suggested, in his best Dracula voice.

"That wasn't funny."

"Sorry. Just trying to bring a little humour into our gloomy lives."

"Is there something you're not telling me?" she asked.

Paul pretended not to have heard her.

"Paul?" Christy snapped at him. "What haven't you told me?"

"Before I say anything, I want you to remember the days when you and I first began seeing each other and you would forgive me anything."

"Go on," she replied stoically.

"You remember when Margaret came over and cleaned the house of whatever spirit was residing here?"

Christy nodded.

"I didn't tell you at the time, but when she left, she was terrified of something. When I asked if she had gotten rid of the ghost, all she could say before charging out of the house was that she had, but that it hadn't been the only one in residence."

Christy looked at him in amazement.

"Wouldn't that have been worth mentioning to me at the time?" Christy asked.

"I didn't want to worry you. I was hoping that, with the lady ghost gone, you'd be able to finally start enjoying the house and actually recover from the events of the past six weeks."

"At least your heart was in the right place," she sighed.

"Then, when I started having those weird daydreams, or whatever they were, I began to wonder if the two things might be connected. I mean, it seems strange that Margaret talked about us still being haunted and then, shortly afterwards, I started dreaming of mothers eating their young."

"Seriously?" she asked, shocked.

"Just a figure of speech," Paul replied.

"No, I'm not buying it," Christy said, shaking her head. "Emma's spirit may have been here when we first moved in, but we haven't seen any signs of an actual haunting since she left, have we? I mean, apart from your dreams?"

Paul was giving her one of those questioning looks he usually used when he felt she had not made a good enough case.

"What?" she asked.

"The kitchen drawer opened by itself again, and something in the mirror bit me," he whispered, trying not to sound completely deranged.

"Where? Let me see," she insisted.

"It was on the wrist, but there's nothing there now. I really think there may be a different presence here. Wouldn't that explain a lot?"

"Absolutely not. I've agreed with you on one spirit. I'm not accepting that there's another one haunting us without some actual proof."

"You do realise that you can't have absolute proof of everything in life?" Paul stated.

"I'm a solicitor, of course I can."

"All right, what would you consider proof?" he asked.

"Something tangible. I don't know, maybe if it could move this pen a few inches."

Christy placed a pen in the centre of the table. The two

stared at it in complete silence for five minutes.

"It appears not to want to make its presence known," she said, almost sarcastically.

"Maybe we have to ask," Paul suggested. "There are probably some rules we should be following."

"Go on then," Christy said. "Ask away."

Paul closed his eyes and bowed his head, feeling completely ridiculous.

"If you can hear me, please let your presence be known," he said, in a slow monotone voice.

They waited, but nothing happened. Finally, Christy got to her feet.

"This has been wonderful fun, but I have to see to dinner."

*

Conversation during their meal was clipped and superficial. Despite her lack of belief in the second spirit, Christy could not seem to take her eyes of the pen.

Once Paul had finished the last morsel on his plate, he sat back and patted his stomach.

"That was delicious," he said.

"All I did was cook some pasta and throw on some ready-made pesto. Hardy a lot of effort."

"It was still..." Paul began.

The entire house shook. It only lasted for a split second, but it had been long enough to make the chandelier above the table swing back and forth in response.

"What the hell was that?" Paul exclaimed.

"I have no idea," Christy replied, as she stared up at the light fixture.

"I hope it wasn't an earthquake. Those things scare the hell out of me."

"You know what really scares the hell out of me?" Christy said, in a weak, shaky voice.

"What?"

Christy pointed to the centre of the table.

The pen was gone.

CHAPTER 25

Christy was trying to climb the fold-down steps to the loft, but every time she got more than two rungs up, they turned soft and rubbery, and she could no longer get a footing. That did not stop her from trying. Something was driving her to get up there. In the dream, she desperately needed to verify what she was too terrified to accept. After trying countless times to gain purchase and failing, she attempted one last manoeuvre. She ran towards the steps, and instead of climbing up one rung at a time, she leapt halfway up and pushed her legs down on the rung with so much force that she was able to get her hands over the top of the hatchway lip.

She pulled herself up into the darkness, then reached for the string light switch. Instead of the usual warm glow from the single bulb, the attic was bathed in a dark purple wash. She stared at the bulb. Somehow, it had transformed into a UV light. Christy took a moment to orientate herself. She had to work out which low wall along the perimeter of the loft was the one she was looking for; the one behind which the possible remains of Emma Barnes had been concealed for over a hundred and fifty years.

Standing up as best she could under the angled joists,

she tried to keep her head low in order to avoid the endless iridescent and intricate cobwebs that adorned the ceiling of the cramped loft. Looking down, she noticed a series of footprints travelling along the plywood walkways. The prints were all the same size, and Christy somehow knew that they belonged to a woman. Under the UV light, the prints glistened as if encrusted with fine diamond dust.

Christy followed them, and quickly discovered that they led from the hatchway to a strange wall, no more than two metres tall. A single brick had been removed from the bottom, and a pale beam of grey light shone from the hole, casting a shadowy illumination onto the dusty wooden flooring.

As Christy approached, she saw a shadow pass across the weak glow from somewhere on the other side of the wall. She should have been terrified, but instead, all she could feel was excitement.

"I don't know if you can hear me," she whispered, as she knelt by the hole. "But I'm here to try and help you."

The grey light pulsed once.

"Does that mean you can understand me?" Christy asked.

The light pulsed again.

Christy lay flat against the wall and slowly eased her hand through the opening. She could not feel anything unusual, and the light did not seem to react. She slid her entire forearm through the hole.

"Please hold my hand, if you can."

Christy gasped as she felt a warmth envelop her hand and wrist. Something was gently clinging to her. Then, the pressure increased. At first, Christy took it to be a show of intensity from the other side, but as the being's grip grew stronger, it began to hurt. Within seconds, Christy felt a searing pain, almost as if her hand was on fire, and the pain quickly became agonising. Christy pulled, but she could not retrieve her arm, so she tried to manoeuvre her body, eventually managing to get her feet up against the wall.

Pushing furiously against the brickwork, she fell backwards as her limb was finally released. She stared at her arm. All that remained of her wrist and hand were blackened skeletal bones, except for the diamond and aquamarine engagement ring on her finger. She looked closer. The same grey light seemed to be pulsing within the pale blue centre of the stone.

Christy opened her eyes, on the verge of screaming, when she felt the warmth of Paul sleeping next to her. Why was Paul in the loft? She looked down at her hand. The strange ring had gone and everything else was intact. She took a deep breath to calm herself, but it still took a few moments for her to process that she had only been dreaming. Snuggling up against Paul, she felt herself drift off again, her dream this time featured a far less stressful encounter between Maggie and a talking deer.

Christy stirred as Paul extricated himself from bed and shuffled down the hall towards the bathroom. She was too exhausted to fully open her eyes and drifting back into the dream about Maggie and the deer, she eventually sensed Paul return to the room and slide back into the bed beside her. Christy smiled as his arms enveloped her upper body. She could feel how chilled he was after the minutes he had spent away from the warmth of their duvet. Even his breath on the back of her neck was strangely cold. She also thought she could detect the smell of stale lager.

The sound of the toilet flushing echoed through the house.

"It's time for daddy to show you how much he loves you," a deep gravelly voice whispered in her ear, as she felt a pair of hands travel down her body.

Christy flew out of bed just as Paul was trying to sneak into the room without waking her. They collided in the dark.

"Jesus!" Paul yelped.

Christy turned on the main light then spun around, glaring at the bed. It was dishevelled but empty. They both turned as they heard pounding paws charging down the hallway. Maggie tore past them, leapt forth from the doorway, and landed on Paul's side of the bed. She began dancing in circles and growling at the bed linen, before suddenly stopping and positioning herself for a wee. Christy called for her to stop, and thankfully she did, though it was obvious that she desperately wanted to continue. Paul grabbed her gently by the collar and led her out of the room. They watched as she sullenly walked the length of the hallway, then disappeared down the stairs.

"I think our dog has developed superpowers," Paul stated.

"Why do you think that?"

"She seems intent on saving us through the heroic use of bowel and bladder."

Christy could not help but smile.

"So, what was it? A nightmare?" Paul asked knowingly.

"I guess so... it's just... I could have sworn it was real."

"I know the feeling. I've had a few of those."

"You go back to bed," Christy said with a sigh. "I'm changing my clothes."

"Do you want to tell me about it?" Paul asked.

"Not now. Maybe in the morning. For the moment, I don't even want to think about it."

Paul stroked her arm, causing her to cringe away from him.

"That's new," he said with concern.

"I'll tell you about it the morning."

She waited until Paul was back in bed, then turned off the overhead light, feeling her way to the wardrobe and rummaging for the light switch. She flicked it on, then screamed.

In the centre of the wardrobe was an old chrome-framed NHS wheelchair. The logo was partially covered by a mismatched piece of nylon that had been used to patch the seat-back.

Paul was out of bed in less than a second, and swiftly moved her away from the wardrobe door. It took him a moment to understand what he was seeing, as a few tendrils of black smoke rose from the centre of the room and drifted upwards. He followed the smoke with his eyes, and quickly realised that the entire ceiling was a swirling mass of roiling black matter. It was neither mist nor fog, but seemed to have characteristics of both.

Despite its appearance, the mass still appeared to have weight to it. There was nothing human about it, but as Paul stared into it, he could feel sentient emotions. They were all scrambled together, but two stood out.

Anger and hate.

"What did you see in here?" he gestured into the wardrobe.

Christy shook her head.

"Because what I'm looking at is a black cloud thing that's covering the ceiling."

"I saw my father's wheelchair," Christy whispered.

"When did you last see the real thing?" Paul asked.

"When I dropped it back at the hospital in Southampton," Christy replied.

"Have a look again and tell me if you can still see it," he asked, with forced calm.

It was obvious that she did not want to look, but also knew she had to. Leaning against Paul, she looked inside. He sensed her body relax.

"There's nothing there."

"Look up."

She slowly raised her eyes.

"Nothing there either," she said with relief.

"Bearing in mind that I have no idea what the hell is going on here, I'm going to hazard a guess that we might just have another haunting problem."

"You think?" she replied sarcastically. She tried to sound strong and in control, but inside, her mind was feeling dangerously fragile.

"Why don't you grab a few things, and we'll go and stay in a hotel for the night. We can decide what our next step will be tomorrow, when it's daytime and the creepiness is at a minimum."

"We can't go to a hotel," Christy reminded him. "There isn't a dog friendly place for miles. Besides, it's after three in the morning. I'm sure we can survive another few hours until sunrise. But if you wouldn't mind, I think I'd prefer to stay downstairs in the newer part of the house."

"Sounds good to me. I doubt there's going to be much more sleeping going on tonight anyway. Want me to make a pot of coffee?"

"Yes please."

Paul started to head out of the room.

"Where the hell do you think you're going?" she asked in a panicked voice.

"Downstairs to make coffee. You said you..."

"Rule number one of fright house is that we stay together. Nobody wanders off. Got it?" Christy stated.

"Got it."

"Good. You wait right there until I put on some clothes, then we can go downstairs together."

"Isn't the final rule of fright house that nobody can ever talk about fright house?" Paul recalled.

"Don't be an ass."

CHAPTER 26

They made camp in the sitting room, then headed into the kitchen, where Christy watched Paul make a jumbo cafetière of French Roast coffee. Opening the cupboard just above his head, Paul gestured to a box of dark chocolate ginger biscuits. Christy nodded without much enthusiasm, taking the biscuits through to the sitting room. The moment she stepped out of the kitchen, the cutlery drawer opened. A single cockroach stepped onto the countertop and stared at Paul, its antennae twitching excitedly.

Paul acted reflexively, grabbing the tea towel hanging off the oven door. In one smooth motion, he spun the material into a tight roll and flicked one end at the insect. Indiana Jones could not have been more accurate, and the bug promptly vanished into a golden mist.

"You alright?" Christy called from the sitting room.

"Yeah. Just tidying up."

Paul finished making the coffee and brought a tray into the sitting room.

Christy refused to talk about her dream or seeing the wheelchair; although they both realised that it may have been the result of something much more complicated than a nightmare, she had no intention of discussing it until the

214

sound of her father's voice next to her in their bed had faded into a far distant memory.

"So, what do you want to talk about?" Paul asked, as he placed the tray on the coffee table. "I know which topics are not allowed, but I'm a little unclear as to which ones are still permitted."

"Obviously we have to talk about this," Christy said, as she patted the sofa cushion next to her. "Suffice to say, when you left the bed to go to the loo, someone else took your place."

"What do mean, someone took my place?" Paul said, with a mixture of fear, anger and maybe even a little jealousy.

Christy gave him her best 'it'll come to you' look.

It took Paul a few moments.

"Oh shit," he said, as the penny finally dropped. "God, I'm so sorry."

He sat next to her and tried to take her hand. She gently moved it away.

"For obvious reasons, I don't think I want to be touched at the moment. I'm still pretty scared and revolted by the whole thing."

"Understandably," Paul said, as he plunged the coffee press. "I shouldn't have left you alone."

"That's not fair on you. We had no idea that something like that could happen. It's as if the spirit can read our minds."

"I don't think there's any doubt about that, whatsoever," Paul agreed. "All the hallucinations I've been having tap into my worst phobias. The cockroaches, the dead plants... all of those are things that have given me the creeps since I was a child."

"But I could actually feel him," Christy insisted. "I could smell his breath, for God's sake."

"Christy, love, I desperately want to make you feel safe, but I'm out of my depth here."

Instead of reaching for him, Christy gently punched him in the arm. That was as physical as they could be at that moment.

"What are we going to do?" she asked.

"We could put the house up for sale?"

"Then what? Trick some other family into moving in with... whatever the hell it is? What if the next buyer has children? Could you seriously see yourself putting them at risk? Before we start making decisions about what to do next with the house, we need to see if we can deal with the problem ourselves. Then, when we're successful, we can decide whether to stay or go."

"What if we aren't successful?"

"That isn't an option," Christy stated.

"Then what do you suggest?" Paul asked. "There's little doubt that these occurrences—"

"Occurrences?" Christy asked, interrupting. "Is that what we're calling them?"

"Why not?" he shrugged. "Do you have a better name for having the shit scared out of you?"

"I guess not," Christy conceded. "I think we should call a professional spiritualist first thing tomorrow and see what they can do to help. In the meantime, we've only got a few hours till dawn. I'm sure we can put up with whatever

216

nastiness it throws at us till then."

"I hate to point this out, but whatever entity we are dealing with is not a night-shift only kind of ghost. The cockroach attack and the mirror thing both happened during the day."

"That may be so, however, I don't know about you, but I will personally feel far less terrified when the sun comes up."

"We'll see," Paul said, unconvinced.

"That's my brave boy," Christy said, patting his knee.

"Shall I try and find something cheerful on TV. Maybe a movie?" Paul suggested.

"Might as well. Perhaps a comedy would be best."

Paul grabbed the Sky remote and went directly to the movie guide. As he scrolled through the grid, he quickly realised that there was something wrong with the menu. He scrolled all the way through the list, but every channel, at every time slot, appeared to be showing a movie called 'The Haunting at Croft House'. He turned to see if Christy had noticed, and was relieved to see that she was staring down at her iPad.

He was about to turn the TV off when Christy spoke.

"Don't you want to see what it's about?" she asked.

"What?"

"I saw the selection. Turn it on. We should at least know what the story is."

Paul chose the first listing he could see, and clicked the select button. The film had already started. It was dark and very grainy, but they were still able to recognise the interior of their house as a single Steadicam moved from the kitchen to the sitting room. It was empty. The camera then tracked to the front of the house where a man, a woman and a black dog were frantically trying to unlock the front door. The pair did not look exactly like Paul and Christy, but seemed to be a generic representation of them. The black Labrador was a close copy of Maggie, but her features, as with the two humans, lacked detail.

Paul paused the image, then tried changing channels, but no matter what he scrolled to, the same movie was paused at the same place. He pressed play, and the two continued watching the television, while Maggie watched them.

The couple on the screen were still battling with the door locks. When they finally managed to open them, they stepped out into pelting rain, descending from a jet-black sky. The woman opened the back door of a car that looked not too dissimilar to theirs, and the Maggie lookalike jumped inside. The man started the vehicle, and as soon as the woman climbed inside, he put the car in gear and sped down the drive. A dense fog was concealing the gap in the huge hedge. As they neared the road, the fog swirled away, revealing a massive iron gate. The two halves were chained and padlocked together where they met in the centre of the drive.

The man jumped out of the car and tried to move the chains and the gates. Neither gave an inch. The camera panned up, revealing that the gates were well over five metres tall, and had been designed to be unclimbable. The woman and dog joined him at the gate, and after a brief discussion, they began to run alongside the hedge, looking

218

for some hole or gap they could climb through. They found that the entire property was ringed not just by the hedge but by thorny brambles that had grown within it to at least three or four metres in height.

The couple looked at each other, then the camera panned to the only part of the property where the hedge and brambles were not barring them from escaping. Running towards the woods at the back of the house, they entered the solid, almost cloying darkness that hung beneath the trunks and branches of the oaks. After a few paces, they noticed a grey glow emanating from one particular tree. As they approached it in the dim light, they realised that the tree was surrounded by a mushroom circle.

Paul stared at the TV in horror. The image was far too close to what he had seen in his dream, though the mushrooms were much bigger than they had been in his vision. Each one looked to be over ten centimetres wide.

The Labrador sniffed at one of them then dropped to the ground and began pawing its nose. The couple started to back away from the old oak, but the mushrooms started to move within the rich loamy soil. At that moment, they realised that they were not mushrooms at all, but rather partially buried skulls. The woman screamed as a skeletal hand reached up through the ground and grabbed her ankle.

The movie cut to a shot taken from the outside of the wooded area. The woods looked dark and ominous. The sound of the woman's scream was joined by the man crying for help in a voice that sounded as if it was gasping for air.

The dog emerged from the darkness. It looked disorientated. It stopped in the middle of the back lawn, looked up into the rainy sky and howled piteously.

Between the trees, where the darkness was blacker than black, dozens of slanted yellow eyes flicked open and stared back towards the house.

They were not the eyes of anything human.

The picture froze and the end credits began to roll. Every credit said exactly the same thing.

IN MEMORY
OF
CHRISTY CHAPPELL
&
PAUL CHAPPELL

"Try the phone," Christy whispered.

Paul tried to use his mobile, but as usual, they had no signal. Christy passed him the landline. He tried 999, but got nothing, just an endless, monotone ringing. Grabbing the phone, Christy tried her office number to see if that would work, putting the landline onto speaker phone so they could both hear. It picked up after the fifth ring. They had expected to hear Christy's message, but instead, all they heard was the howl of the wind and trees rustling, until a deep, hollow voice crackled through the receiver.

"I'm sorry, but since the untimely death of Christy and Paul Chappell, this line is no longer in service."

The two of them looked at each other in horror. The dynamics had changed. They were not just experiencing individual hallucinations. It was now a shared experience; the entity seemed to be getting better at manipulating their minds.

Paul got to his feet and started for the front door.

"Do you think that's a good idea?" Christy asked, in little more than a whisper.

"Probably not. Are you coming?"

Christy followed him. Maggie was about to join them, but Christy signalled for her to stay in the sitting room. Paul reached the front door and looked to Christy for moral support. He tried opening the door.

It would not budge.

"Great," Christy murmured.

Paul tried everything to release it, but the door held fast. He was about to try and ram it with his shoulder when Christy stepped in his way and grabbed an unusual looking key from the bowl by the door.

"We've never used that," Paul pointed out.

"We've never been haunted before," she shot back.

Inserting the slender key in a morticed security lock at the very top of the door, she tried to turn it. The lock was stiff, but eventually, it gave in to her demands, accompanied by a metal-on-metal squeal. Christy tried the door handle again. The door swung open. Rain was tipping down and the sky was pure obsidian.

They did not even bother with the car; they were starting to trust the authenticity of the film's narrative. They only needed to walk halfway down their drive to see that there was no means of exit: a massive iron gate was blocking the driveway. The two halves were hinged to huge stone pillars, and a rusted chain and vintage padlock bound them together.

"But we don't have a bloody gate," Paul shouted above the noise of the wind and rain.

"We do now," Christy shouted back.

"Do you want to check out the woods," Paul asked.

"No. Do you?" she replied, without any hesitation.

"Not particularly. I suggest we go back inside. I have a feeling that we might be safer in there than out here."

"I hope you're right."

She took his arm as they plodded back towards the open front door, but just as they neared the entrance, it started to swing shut. Paul and Christy used all their strength to push against it. Maggie ran into the hall and could be heard barking furiously at something. The dog suddenly cried out as if she had been struck. Whether because of their parental concern for Maggie or the adrenaline that was surging through them both, they managed to get the door far enough open so they both could lunge through.

They landed in a crumpled, sodden pile in the hallway. Maggie began licking them both, trying in her own way to offer some support. Christy noticed that she did not seem to want to put pressure on her right front paw.

"I think she's broken her foot," Christy said, holding up Maggie's front paw. The Labrador whined in pain.

"Or something else broke it," Paul murmured. "I'm going to put her in the utility room. Hopefully she'll be out of harm's way in there."

"It sounds like you're expecting things to get a lot more complicated."

"Aren't you?"

"But why? What have we done?"

"Well, as far as he knows, if it is in fact a he, we are living in his house, and I'm fairly sure he can sense that we plan to take down that wall in the loft."

"I didn't know that we had that plan," Christy said.

"We do now."

"If this 'he' you are referring to is Emma's late husband, what makes you think that he is going to let us do that?"

"I don't know what he can do to stop us. He can only use dreams and hallucinations as far as I can tell."

"Even just with those he's been doing a pretty good job," she replied. "What about the front door? That wasn't a dream. Something was closing it on us."

"We had better just hope that was his one big party trick."

Christy looked at her husband doubtfully.

Suddenly, they both heard a squeaking noise coming from the back of the house.

"What fresh hell is this?" Paul asked no one in particular.

"I know that sound," Christy said, as icy chills ran up her spine.

The noise grew louder. It wasn't just a squeak, it was more of a thump-squeak, pause, thump-squeak, pause. She had heard that sound every day for the past however many weeks, until the second stroke had finished off the culprit. She got to her feet and stepped out of the hallway, looking towards the sitting room.

Her father's ancient wheelchair moved towards them, Christy's father slouched within it.

CHAPTER 27

Christy stood transfixed as she stared at the figure in the wheelchair. Just like in the Haunting of Croft House film they had just watched, there was something wrong with the detail. It definitely looked like her father, but at the same time, it did not. The face lacked his characteristic sharp, unflattering angles, and it struck her that whoever or whatever had whipped up the grotesque double, they had made one big mistake.

They had paralysed the wrong side of him.

Paul tried to pull her away, but she shook him off.

"It's not him," she whispered. She glared at the faulty apparition. "I said it's not him," she shouted.

The man and the chair began to shake. Gently at first, but then the shaking became violent. The image began to distort, seeming to almost drift out of phase. The illusion doubled like a drunk's eye view. Then, it was gone. The room went back to normal. Christy felt a sense of pride at having been able to confront the hallucination.

"What the hell was that?" Paul asked.

"That was it trying to get into my head. It's going to have to do a lot better than that," she replied.

The lights went off throughout the house, and a thin,

reedy voice drifted towards them.

"Chrissy?" the voice whispered.

It sounded weak, as though it were unable to gather enough strength to speak.

"Bunny?"

Christy staggered backwards, grabbing Paul to stop herself from falling. There were a few people in her life who had called her Chrissy, but only one person in the entire world had ever called her Bunny.

Christy had been five years old, and she and her mother had spent the morning watching 'Bambi' on the television. It had been the first time Christy had ever seen the film, and for the rest of the day, and the ten days that followed, she hopped around their Southampton house, wiggling her nose whenever she spoke. Her mother, amused by her daughter's adorable antics, had started called her Bunny, which had made the little girl twitch her nose with even more enthusiasm.

Unfortunately, on the eleventh day, 'Bunny' had accidently knocked into her father while he had been reading his morning copy of The Sun. Hungover and in a foul mood, Ralph had shoved his daughter roughly out of the way.

"Grow up," he had snarled, before returning to an article about Sandy, who liked sports and having fun, on page three of the paper.

Christy's mother had not intervened, for fear of what he might do to her or their daughter, and Christy had never play acted again. But the private nickname had stuck, though it had only ever been used when Ralph was out of

226

the house.

Paul was about to switch on his iPhone light, but before he could press the icon, an eerie spotlight appeared, shining directly above an old, worn-out looking hospital bed.

"Jesus," he gasped.

Captured in the illumination was an old woman, bound to the rickety metal framed bed. She was painfully thin, and her features were drawn back in an emaciated leer. Open sores were visible on her face and restrained arms; some looked old, and were caked in blackening scabs, while others oozed a yellowish-green pus. Her eyes were sunken so far back into her skull that it was hard to imagine that they were still even remotely functional.

"Mum?" Christy asked, in little more than a whisper.

"Is that you, Bunny?" the woman replied weakly, revealing rotten teeth imbedded in dead, blackened gums.

"What happened to you?" Christy murmured, as she started to approach the bed.

"Why did you never come looking for me?" the woman cried out. "You were all I had, and you never came for me."

Tears were streaming down Christy's face.

"I didn't know that you wanted me to. I only just found the letter a few days ago."

"This is what I've become," the woman croaked. "This is what you have made me. If only you had cared enough to look for me..."

Christy was about to run to her, but Paul grabbed her tightly and turned her towards him.

"That thing is not your mother," he said, looking deep into her eyes. "It's just another hallucination. It's deliberately trying to hurt you so it can feed on your pain."

"But she's right. I never did look for her. She must have needed me so badly."

Christy started to turn back to the bed.

Paul forced her behind him, then ran directly at the hallucination. He was only centimetres away when the woman in the bed sprang to her feet, dropping the bedclothes around her. She was naked and terrifyingly neglected. She looked like a one-hundred-year-old cadaver. Paul tried not to stare.

"What's the matter, Little Paulie Poo Pants?" the woman cackled. "Going to cry and run home to mummy?"

"You're not real!" he screamed.

The old woman shrieked with laughter.

"You can't hurt me," Paul shouted at her.

"Little Paulie Poo Pants, Little Paulie Poo Pants, it wiggles in his shorts when he tries to dance!" she recited.

The taunting that he had received in his pre-school days after an 'accident' during play-time had been buried so deep within his mind that he had never even considered that those words would hurt him again. He was wrong; the taunt felt just as painful and fresh as it had done when he was five years old.

"Fuck you," he shouted at the image, before lunging straight at it.

The spotlight extinguished, and Paul fell though empty air. Landing hard on the carpeted hallway, he shakily got to his feet and turned towards where he knew Christy was standing. Retrieving his phone, he activated the light. Christy's face lit up, except it was not her face. It was the face of the woman in the bed.

"How does it feel, knowing that you've been fucking her mother all this time?" the woman screamed at him.

Paul ignored what his eyes were seeing and stepped towards Christy, wrapping his arms around her. He could feel her crying as he held her. He pulled back and shone the light on her face.

The old woman was gone.

In that moment, all the lights came back on, making them both jump.

"Are you alright?" he asked Christy, as he held her hands in his.

"Not really," she replied, shaking her head. "That was all a little bit too real."

"Did you hear the last part?" Paul asked.

"When you said 'fuck you' to a ghost?" She tried to smile.

"I've always had a way with words." He smiled back.

"We can't fight this thing," Christy whispered.

"Yes, we can. I just proved it. We've just got to ignore whatever it throws at us. It can only create images. They're not real."

"What about the gate across our driveway?" she asked. "That seemed real enough?"

Paul had to ponder that for a moment.

"I think it can manifest its power to make something appear real, even though we know it's not. The gate felt real because our brains told us it was real. It's the same as when it was pushing the door closed. It couldn't have really been doing that. I don't think it can actually create tangible objects or move real things. It's simply able to mess with our heads to the extent that we believe those situations are real."

"What about Maggie's foot. Something did that to her."

"Maybe she did it to herself, trying to get away from something that was scaring her," Paul suggested.

"I hope you're right," Christy answered.

They heard something crash against the nearest wall. Shards of crystal shrapnel scattered in every direction.

"Was that our vase?" Christy asked, frightened. "What happened to all of this being in our heads?"

"It is in our heads. Could I do this if it were real?" Paul bent over and grabbed a savage looking piece of broken glass. "Shit," he yelped, as it cut his hand.

He looked at Christy with an expression of complete shock and disbelief.

"I was so sure..."

Paul never finished his sentence, as the bright orange pottery cat that Christy had made as a child and had, after deep deliberation, left back at the Southampton house, struck him on his right temple.

He crumpled to the ground like a wet towel.

"Paul!" Christy screamed.

CHAPTER 28

Christy managed to drag Paul out of the hallway and into the old sitting room. She laid him on his back and tried to revive him, to no avail. Grabbing her phone, she tried to call for help, but there was no signal, and the internet was down.

Tapping Paul's smart watch, she checked his vitals. Other than a fast heart rate, all the readings were normal. Relieved, she dashed into the sitting room, returning with a pillow and blanket, and after making him as comfortable as possible, she kissed his forehead.

"Wish me luck," she whispered.

Christy knew exactly what she had to do. Everything that had happened since they had moved in all related back to one thing. The wall in the loft. Something was behind it. She had no plan as such, which was probably a good thing. She was starting to feel as if the entity knew what they were going to do before they did.

Before heading upstairs, she checked on Maggie in the utility room, making sure that she had enough food and water to last should something bad happen. She then rummaged in Paul's toolbox and found herself a large hammer and a blunt looking chisel. Placing the items in a hessian shopping bag, she added Paul's favourite rubber-coated, tactical, military-grade torch.

After giving Maggie one last scratch between the ears, she moved slowly towards the stairs. As she neared the doorway, the lights within the house began to shimmer, and she could feel the house shaking slightly as she mounted the first step. With each upward climb, the shimmering of the lights became more abrupt, and she could hear some of them sizzling as the surge increased. One of the two lights above the stairs sparked dramatically, before they died completely.

Still only halfway up, Christy saw a shadow pass across the landing at the top of the stairs. Determined not to be caught out, she took the last few steps two at a time, trying to locate what could have caused the greyed out silhouette she had just seen. There was no one there.

Running to the ceiling hatch, she looked up at the sealed cover, and a momentary wave of panic washed over her. She had never opened the thing herself, Paul had always done it, and in her current mental state, all memory of what he had done had disappeared. Slowing her breathing, Christy tried to recall what he had told her. An image of the guest room wardrobe floated into her mind. Yes. She remembered now. Paul had hidden the ladder release tool in the guest room.

She ran down the hallway and into the nearest room, but the moment she stepped inside, the door slammed shut behind her with enough force to crack the solid pine door down the middle. She spun around. The old man from the pub garden was standing against the closed door.

"What are you doing here?" she asked, trying to remain calm.

He looked confused, then a smile spread across his face. His mouth was too big; his teeth too sharp, and Christy realised that it was not the old man standing in front of her at all. It was Geoffrey Barnes, turning one of her own memories against her.

"Enough!" she screamed. "Stop hiding behind my memories. If you're going to do this, show me who you really are."

The man stared at her, then began to change. His body thickened and grew taller; his old tweeds became a black, woollen suit; his face became younger but heavier. Thick, mutton chop sideburns sprouted on his pasty face, and his hair darkened, brushing itself back from his forehead. He stared at Christy with hate and curiosity.

As she looked closely at the form of Geoffrey Barnes, she noticed that the outline of his body was uneven, and in places indistinct. It was as if some painter had focused all of their talent on the centre of the canvas and had left the edges incomplete.

Christy reached into the wardrobe and removed a long stick with a brass hook on the end. She turned back to the apparition and began to smile, then laugh, pointing directly at Geoffrey's face.

"You're what we've been so scared of? You're nothing but an angry, pathetic little man, who spent his whole life trying to convince the world that he was someone worth remembering. Someone important. But everyone saw right through you, didn't they? Even poor Emma, in the end.

Eight years she stayed by your side, waiting for your big break, but it never came, did it? Her life with you had become a nightmare. Everything about you repulsed her. Your pitiful fumbling in bed could never satisfy her. She pretended it did, but she was waiting. Waiting for someone like the bricklayer's apprentice to make her feel alive; to awaken the feelings and emotions that had laid dormant for so long."

Christy had no idea where this passionate speech had come from. It just flowed from her like some long-supressed outpouring of bilious scorn.

The phantom staggered backwards as his image began to dissipate, drifting halfway through the closed guest bedroom door. Christy grabbed the handle and swung the door open, right through the other half of Geoffrey's diminishing form.

Running back down the hallway, she fitted the hook through the ring at one end of the hatch cover and pulled. The cover swung open, and the ladder dropped halfway to the floor. Christy unfolded the rest of it, then started up towards the loft.

Something made her look down, and she saw Geoffrey glaring up at her. The apparition seemed more solid again, as if he had regained some of his strength since Christy's verbal assault. His mouth was opening and closing, but she could not hear any sound. It was as if he could only speak through his hallucinations, not as himself.

Ignoring him, she made her way over the hatchway lip and onto the plywood flooring. She switched on the overhead light, but the bulb blew instantly, sending glass shards everywhere. Reaching into the hessian bag, she removed Paul's torch and pushed the base. A beam of bright white light cut through the darkness like forked lightening. Christy scanned the perimeter of the loft, looking for some clue as to which wall she needed to target. She froze the light on the one she had seen in her dream. The dust at the base of the wall had clearly been disturbed.

Easing herself under the angled joists, while making sure that she only stepped on the wooden walkways, she slowly made her way towards the wall, occasionally turning and shining the torch behind her. When she had almost reached her destination, a strange sound from behind prompted her to turn again, just in time to see a thin black leg rising through the hatchway. A second, then a third limb appeared, taking hold of the hatchway lip and pulling the rest of the creature's body into the attic.

Christy was momentarily frozen in place. The spider was the size of a large dog, its body almost filling the square opening as it hoisted itself up. Once inside the loft, its black, bulging eyes scanned the room, locking on Christy. Some deep-rooted strength shocked her out of her fear-induced immobility, and she turned back to the wall, dumping the contents of the bag onto the floor. She grabbed the hammer and chisel and began smashing the mortar between the other bricks.

Christy could hear the pitter patter of the spiders legs creeping towards her along the plywood walkway, but refused to look back, focusing her mind on her task. She managed to remove three more bricks from the bottom row, then began to hammer the next row up. As they no

235

longer had any support from below, the bricks loosened easily.

Lying on her back, Christy pushed against the swaying wall with her feet, but as it started to give, she sensed that something had changed within the loft. Grabbing the torch, she turned, ready to square off against the giant arachnid, before quickly realising that it was not alone.

The spider was standing above the prone figure of Paul, who was lying motionless on the floor. As Christy tried to work out how he got up there and what to do, the spider lowered itself to the ground and bit into Paul's neck. Christy turned away, just about manging to hold back a scream, and began smashing at the wall with everything she had. Suddenly, with no lower support, an entire section collapsed, revealing a jagged opening almost a meter wide.

Without hesitation, Christy climbed through the gap, using the torch to reveal what lay beyond. The space was empty, save for a tattered looking old rug that had been rolled up and pushed into the crevice where the roof met the attic floor. Christy grabbed one end of the rug and dragged it out into the open space. As she was about to unroll it, the entire house shook violently, and she heard the spider let out an horrific, high-pitched scream. Her hand suddenly felt as if it was on fire, and Christy looked down to discover that the torch was glowing red and smoking. Shocked, she let it fall to the floor, whereupon the glass lens smashed. Seconds later, the LED light went out.

The small space was plunged into complete darkness, and Christy felt a wave of panic wash over her, threatening to reduce her to nothing more than a terrified girl, waiting for the sound of her father's footsteps on the landing. Closing her eyes, she began to retreat into herself, but there was a force pushing against her panic. Something inside her was rebelling, and the more she tried to escape her fear, the more it pushed back against her. Suddenly, like a rubber band stretched too tightly, something inside Christy snapped.

She opened her eyes and glared at the darkness. This time, she was not going to be the victim. She was not going to let the ghost of Geoffrey Barnes leave her quivering in terror. She was going to fight back. Looking down, she identified the outline of the rug in the gloom, and as she continued to fix her gaze on the object, the room grew brighter, a strange grey glow emanating from the rug's two ends. Slowly, gently, Christy unfurled it across the floor.

The bones of Emma Barnes rattled free from their prison, alongside a few scraps of leather, a couple of carved bone buttons, and the aquamarine and diamond ring that Christy had seen in her dream. It was the ring that was emitting the grey light, enshrouding the remains of the woman in a soft, pale radiance.

Christy began to cry, her tears a mixture of sadness at seeing the vestiges of Geoffrey's vengeful rage and joy at having finally found the young woman, whose remains could now be blessed and interred as they should have been all those years previously.

A man screamed violently from beyond the wall, and Christy heard heavy footsteps climbing the loft ladder. Turning to face the onslaught, she noticed the grey light brighten as it took on a wispy form, before passing through the hole in the wall and wafting towards the hatchway. As Geoffrey's head began to emerge through the opening, the nebulous grey light stopped, expanding and lengthening upwards. The details were far too ephemeral to ever solidify into something recognisable, but Christy thought she could almost make out the translucent outline of a woman, and she knew in her heart that she was looking at the newly released spirit of Emma.

Geoffrey's apparition suddenly evaporated into its dark, smoke-like form, and as if pushed by a sudden gust of wind, the smoke dropped down to the bottom of the ladder. Christy watched in astonishment as Emma's spirit followed, and she was about to run after the pair when she was struck by an inexplicable need to grab the hammer first.

By the time she had climbed down from the loft, Emma's trailing light was passing into the master bedroom. Christy approached cautiously, and as she peered around the doorframe, she found herself listening to one of the strangest sounds she had ever heard in her life. It was coming from the wardrobe, and sounded like whale song that had been sped up and played back through a harmonic sequencer.

It was not the language of the living.

Her fear of the situation was suppressed by her curiosity, and Christy peeked her head around the wardrobe door. Emma's luminous outline was shimmering only inches from her husband's dark, foreboding spirit. The two were standing between the opposing dressing mirrors. The smouldering black mist was distorting, trying to touch Emma's spirit but failing. Suddenly, Emma's form shifted into a vision of her as she had been before her death. Though her transitory form only lasted for a millisecond, Christy could see just how beautiful and strong she had been.

Before the black entity could react, Emma returned to being no more than a grey mist, and streamed into the right-hand mirror. The house was filled with an ungodly roar as Geoffrey's spectre dived into the same reflective surface.

Christy ran into the wardrobe and stood between the two mirrors. She could see the infinity effect and the black, smoke-like force chasing the grey lightness from one reflective image to the next. Christy then remembered the hammer that she had almost unconsciously picked up in the loft. She now knew why she had needed to bring it along. It must have been a final message from Emma. She had always planned to lead her murderous husband into the one realm from which he could never again return. Christy's job was to eliminate any portals on her side.

Raising the hammer, Christy smashed the right mirror, shielding her eyes from the shards, before turning to the other. For a split second, she thought she saw a tendril of dark smoke curling up from the bottom right corner, but before the entity could fully free itself from its glass prison, she destroyed the mirror with one hard swing.

The wardrobe light flickered back to life.

There was no sign of either entity.

All that remained were thousands of shimmering shards of mirror glass.

Christy felt a surge of relief as she dropped the hammer

and ran downstairs. Paul was still lying on the sitting room floor, but his eyes were open. He stared up at her, his expression full of confusion.

"What happened?" he mumbled.

"Don't worry," she replied, taking his hand. "I took care of everything."

CHAPTER 29

Despite it still being early October, an icy breeze bombarded the four people standing in the graveyard of St John's Church, nestled in the tiny village of Ranmoor just outside of Sheffield. The sky was dark and brooding, and though it was only three in the afternoon, the sunlight was so restrained that it felt like dusk had already fallen.

The police had retained Emma's remains for almost two weeks, though once she had been positively identified, a follow-up investigation had been deemed unnecessary, since the culprit was already dead. A medical examiner had informed them that she had most likely been strangled, considering the damage to her hyoid bone, which though hardly surprising, had greatly saddened Christy. Amazingly, the police had also managed to track down one surviving family member, Mary Baker, who lived just outside of Sheffield in a cottage that had been owned by the family for over two hundred years.

When the police had notified the seventy-three-year-old that remains had been found of a very distant relative, they had expected indifference, or maybe even suspicion, but Mary had been fascinated by the news, and had insisted on paying for all funeral costs as well as a burial plot within the church grounds so that Emma would finally lie among some of her family members.

The graveside service was short, but stressed the sadness of a life that had not only been cut short, but had also been forgotten about for so many years. As the coffin descended into the damp Yorkshire soil, Mary tossed in a single white lily. After sharing a few words with Christy and Paul, Mary walked away with the elderly priest, the two of them holding each other up as they made for the old church.

"Are you glad we came?" Christy asked.

"Yes," Paul replied, as he unconsciously felt the scar where the pottery cat had struck him. "I know I was against the idea, but seeing her laid to rest feels only right."

"Agreed. It seems to have finally put a stop on the whole sorry mess."

"I'm not so sure about that..." Paul gestured his head towards the far end of the cemetery.

Standing statue still, watching the pair intensely, was the old man from the pub. He was dressed in the same tweed suit, and did not seem the least bit fazed by the bitter wind.

"I need to talk to him," Christy stated.

"If he has any more to say, he knows where to find us."

Christy searched for the right words.

"I think it's important that I talk to him," she insisted.

Paul watched as Christy made her way over to the old man.

"Nice service," the man said.

"It was you, wasn't it?" Christy asked, in a lowered voice.

"I'm not sure I follow..."

"You were the apprentice, weren't you?"

The old man took a moment to fiddle with his pipe.

"Aye. I was," he replied, his voice laden with sadness.

"Is that why you're still... here... in our time?"

He nodded.

"I couldn't pass on while Emma was stuck in that house. Especially as she was the only one stopping that crazed husband of hers from wreaking havoc on whoever lived there."

"I'm not sure I understand?"

"Her husband didn't die of heart failure. He died from guilt and terror. Emma saw to it that, after what he did to her, she made his life a living hell. When he did eventually drop dead, she made sure that his spirit was kept in a far distant corner of the nether plane. It was only after you thought to rout her spirit from Croft House that his was able to break back into your world again."

"But why didn't her husband just pass on to the next plane himself? Why stay here at all?" she asked.

"Fear. Fear of her remains being discovered. Once that happened, he knew that his good name would be sullied forever."

"And what about you?" Christy asked. "Why haven't you moved on?"

"I stayed, waiting for the day when Emma and me could pass on to the next world together."

"You can do that now, can't you?"

"Aye. I'm hoping we can."

"May I ask you a strange question?"

"I would have thought you'd have considered all of this

to be somewhat strange."

"Did her husband kill you as well?'

"Aye, he did. But only after having me build that blasted wall in the loft. I had no idea what he planned to do with it. He told me he needed it to store something valuable. I did most of the work, then after leaving a gap so he could access the area, he struck me from behind with something hard and heavy. I woke up in the woods behind the house, sat astride his horse with a noose around my neck. He waited for me to be fully awake before slapping the old grey, leaving me hanging from an oak tree. Even killing me wasn't enough for him, and after I'd passed he bled me where I swung, then dismembered me. My body parts are buried at the foot of the oak."

"And you've been waiting all this time?"

"Aye," he replied.

"If you were a young man when you died, why do you appear so old?"

"After I began the vigil of waiting for my Emma, I soon found that folk in the village and at the house seemed more agreeable to my wandering around as the person you see before you. They felt more comfortable with me old, rather than young."

"You don't have to look like that anymore," she said gently. "I'd like to see the real you, before you leave us."

The old man was suddenly filled with emotion, and after brushing away an errant tear, he took a step back, closed his eyes and bowed his head. Christy looked on as the man transformed into a strapping young lad. The old tweeds became a linen shirt, and cotton trousers; the cloth cap became a head of glorious blond hair; his eyes, which had been red rimmed and rheumy, became clear and bright blue.

He smiled once, then vanished into the greying afternoon.

Christy walked back to where Paul was studying some of the older headstones.

"Is he okay?" he asked.

"It looks as if he is now. He confirmed to me that he was the reason Emma was murdered. I just hope the two of them find each other."

"I thought you didn't believe in any of that stuff?"

"I didn't, but considering recent events, I've had to make a few adjustments to my belief system."

Christy kissed her husband on the cheek, and the two made their way across the muddy cemetery to their car.

The two of them hardly spoke during the drive back to Hurst, content to ponder their own thoughts about the happenings of the past few weeks, and once they arrived back at the house, tired and hungry, Christy whipped up a cheese and smoked salmon omelette, while Paul opened a bottle of chilled Chardonnay. Maggie was staying with the Balmfords, as they had not known whether they would end up staying the night up north, so they had the house to themselves.

As they sat down to dinner, Christy let out a heavy sigh.

"I know we promised not to discuss the house until after the funeral..."

"So?" Paul replied, as he did battle with a long strand of melted Gruyere cheese.

"So, the funeral's over. It's time we discussed everything."

"My feelings haven't changed," Paul replied. "I love this house. I know that you've been to hell and back, but I'm happy here. I really don't want to move."

Christy studied him as she took a sip of wine.

"It's taken a lot of mental to-ing and fro-ing, but I think I agree. I keep thinking back to the book, The World According to Garp, you know the part where their house gets hit by a plane? Garp points out to his wife that, after such an unlikely accident, their home is almost certain to remain safe from then on. We've just experienced something even more unlikely, and I feel like this is going to be nothing but a happy house from now on."

"Agreed." Paul smiled, raising his glass. "To Croft House. May she protect us, keep us warm, and enrich our lives."

"Here, here," Christy toasted back. "You know, now that the house is well and truly clear of unwanted guests, there's something we haven't done yet."

"What's that," Paul asked with a mouthful of food.

"If you have to ask, then it obviously isn't that important to you," she replied, with a cheeky grin.

"Oh, that. No, that's very, very important."

"I'm glad to hear it."

Christy leaned across the table to kiss him, but just before their lips touched, there was a loud knock on the door.

Paul begrudgingly got up and walked to the front entrance, opening it with the intention of giving the unexpected visitor a piece of his mind for disturbing them at such an hour.

"I'm really very sorry to bother you so late," Margaret announced. "But I feel I left you both terribly in the lurch after my previous visit."

Paul was almost speechless. The spiritualist had aged at least ten years since she had 'cleansed' the house. Her hair was almost completely white, and looked not to have been in the proximity of a brush for quite some time.

"Why don't you come in?" Christy called from the other room.

Margaret looked horrified.

"I'm fine out here," she replied, a little too quickly. "I just came by to say how sorry I am, and also to see if I could possibly pick up my phone. You mentioned that I left it here when I..."

"Scarpered?" Paul suggested.

"Yes, I suppose I did leave with unusual haste," she conceded.

Christy joined Paul at the front door and looked out at Margaret. It had started to rain and the wind was picking up.

"Oh, for heaven's sake, Margaret, come in and have a glass of wine," Christy offered.

Margaret looked terrified at the very notion of stepping inside.

"The house is completely clean," Paul added.

Margaret gave the pair a doubting look, then held her arms out, with her palms facing upwards. She closed her eyes for a moment, then looked puzzled. Walking inside a little way, she raised her hands again.

"How very odd," she said, as she walked right past the pair and into the hallway, lifting her arms completely over her head and closing her eyes. "It's clean. Your house is completely clean. I don't understand. I thought…"

"You thought what?" Paul interrupted.

"It's just that I…"

"Are you trying to tell us something, Margaret?" Christy asked pointedly. "Or did you intend never to mention the fact that you left us with a worse presence than the one you removed?"

Margaret hung her head.

"I didn't mean to. I had no idea that a second spirit lay dormant within the house. That's why I haven't come by before now. I was terrified to see what had transpired here, but I don't feel any presence at all now. Your home feels completely devoid of any unwanted entities."

"We did have a little bit of a problem initially, but everything is fine now," Christy explained. "Would you like to come in and have a glass of wine?"

"I really shouldn't," Margaret mumbled, as she walked past them and made her way to the sitting room.

Once she was seated, they gave her the entire saga, from the moment she had left to the funeral in Yorkshire. When Paul told her about seeing the man in the churchyard, she visibly paled.

"What's the matter." Christy asked. "You've gone a funny colour."

Margaret took a big swig from her glass of wine.

"The man you described, in the tweeds with the cloth cap… well… I've seen him for as long as I can remember, wandering around the local area."

"Is that a problem?" Paul asked.

"I don't know. I always got a strange sensation whenever I saw him. I even suspected that he might not be one of the living."

"You may have been correct," Paul stated.

"But for a spirit to have remained for all that time and used up so much of its strength to maintain a form as he did…" She bowed her head. "He must have been so very, very lonely."

After Margaret had downed the rest of her wine, they walked her to the front door, and she was about to leave when Christy stopped her.

"Don't forget your phone."

Christy opened a drawer in the hallway table and produced Margaret's sparkly mobile, holding it out to her. She took it with a look of sadness and supressed guilt.

"I feel I could have done more to help," Margaret said.

"I couldn't agree more," Paul replied, as he opened the door for her.

Paul watched her drive her ludicrous little car off into the night while Christy headed back inside. As Margaret swerved onto the lane, Paul saw a young man standing at the bottom of their garden, looking up at the house. He had seen him earlier that same day, in the churchyard.

"You can come in if you want," he called to him.

The young man walked up to the front entrance.

"I feel I should introduce myself," he said, offering his hand to Paul. "My name is Daniel."

"And mine is Paul."

"This house, your house, was the only connection I ever had with her," Daniel said. "Even after she died, I could always count on being able to communicate with her when I visited Croft House. Now that she has no reason to stay on this plane, I wanted to see if there was any trace of her left, so that I could at least have that memory to take with me."

"So, you are moving on?" Paul asked.

"I've no reason to stay here without her, do I? I have been waiting in the light, but she is yet to join me."

"Won't you be together now in... in wherever it is you go?" Paul asked clumsily.

"I was hoping so, but it doesn't always work out that way. She may well have chosen to meet with her family, rather than some daft teenage lad she knew briefly in the last few years of her life."

"I hope you find that she has waited for you," Paul said.

"That's kind of you to say, especially after all the problems you've had to deal with because of us."

"Do you want to come into the house now?"

Daniel looked up at their home and nodded.

Paul held the front door open for him to walk through. Daniel seemed nervous as he stepped into the hallway. Christy appeared, looking at him with apprehension for a moment, before smiling warmly.

"Hello again," she said. "Welcome home."

Daniel had no interest in any part of the house except the loft, so Paul opened the hatch and let him go up alone. The wall that had entombed Emma's remains was gone, and the area had been thoroughly cleaned, with every trace of the wall's existence removed. Daniel only stayed up there for a few minutes, after which he descended the ladder and thanked Christy and Paul for letting him have those few moments within their house.

Paul held the front door open for him.

"I suppose this means we won't be seeing you anymore?" he said.

"We'll see, won't we," the younger version of Daniel replied with a wink, before disappearing down the drive.

CHAPTER 30

The next morning, Christy was up well before dawn. She had big plans for the day, and did not want Paul to have any idea what she was doing. Before stepping out into the light rain, she checked she had her keys, phone and the envelope that Mrs Gillott had slipped into her pocket at her father's funeral.

It was early enough that the morning rush hour had not yet started, and she was hopeful that she would be able to make the trip in under ninety minutes. Pulling out of their drive, she headed off towards Southampton. The route had become awfully familiar during the past few months, but instead of taking her regular exit towards the city, she followed the signs to the A27, heading east.

Roadworks slowed her progress, but with every mile she covered, her excitement grew. A few months ago, she would never have dreamed that this day would come. As far as she was concerned, the book had well and truly been closed after her father's death, yet something about the saga that had unfolded in their new house had unlocked some feelings that she had thought no longer existed.

She turned off at the first Chichester exit, and followed her GPS to 107 King George Gardens. She found an attractive but slightly run down 1930s detached building. It looked as if it had at one time been a residential hotel. She parked on the gravel drive, and after a fortifying breath, walked up to the front door, pressing the doorbell. She heard a distinct ding-dong echo somewhere within the structure, and after a few moments, the inner flap of the wrought iron spy hole opened reluctantly. The eyes of an elderly woman appeared on the other side.

"Yes?" the woman asked abruptly.

"I'm trying to find my mother. All I know is that she lived here about twenty years ago."

Christy heard a number of heavy locks and chains being released before the door opened. The woman had to be in her eighties, and was wearing what had likely been tastefully conservative clothing forty years earlier, but was now worn out, and far too big for her diminished body. She gestured to a hall table that contained new disposable masks in sealed plastic.

Christy put one on as the woman backed away from her.

Christy walked into a nicely proportioned entry hall and could see a large sitting room at the rear of the house. Several women from different age brackets seemed to be gathered for some sort of a meeting. Someone must have sensed Christy's observation because the sitting room door suddenly shut.

"Her name was Alison Burger and..." Christy fumbled for the envelope in her pocket. She withdrew the single sheet of paper on which was written the address in Chichester. "This is all I have. My mother's neighbour held this address for the day when I would want to see her."

"And you waited twenty years?" the woman asked, with clear disapproval. "Anyway, I have no idea why you were given this address. I have lived here for over forty years and have never heard of an Alison Burger, or anyone named anything like that."

"Are you sure?" Christy implored.

"Are you doubting my word, young lady," the old woman scowled. "Perhaps you should leave."

"But I have nowhere else to look. This address was my only hope."

"Perhaps if you'd thought to try a little sooner, you may have had better luck. After twenty years, a trail can grow very cold. I believe that if your mother had wanted to speak with you, she would have found a way to do so."

"But that's the thing," Christy insisted. "She sent me a letter soon after she left, but I only received it recently."

A younger woman, perhaps in her fifties, stepped into the hall.

"Do you need any help, Agnes?"

"I do not, thank you, Eugene. This young lady was about to leave."

As the heavy oak door shut behind her, Christy felt devastated. She had put so much hope in that one snippet of information. Brushing away a tear, she climbed into her car, and was about to start the engine when the other woman from the hallway knocked gently on the driver's side window. Christy lowered it. The woman passed her a small piece of paper that looked to have been torn from a ringed binder.

"It's been long enough," the woman said, as she turned

away and headed back towards the house.

On it were two lines of text. The note looked to have been written in haste.

It said simply:

49 Priory Rd, Chichester
She was known as Alison Ballard

Christy entered the address into Google Maps and drove back into the town, parking less than a hundred yards from the Chichester Festival Theatre, the only place anywhere near the house where she knew for a fact that she would be able to park.

She started down North Street, then cut through St Johns Road to Priory Road. Just past the Quaker Meeting Room was a small group of elegant Georgian town houses. Number forty-nine was the second one. She rang the doorbell and had to wait a long time before someone opened the door.

"May I help you?" a woman in her early sixties asked. She was stylishly dressed and carried herself with calm self-assurance. Her short, brushed-back grey hair still showed some traces of its original blond colour. A simple understated platinum wedding ring was her only visible jewellery.

"I'm looking for my mother. I knew her as Alison Burger, but I believe she changed her name to Ballard," Christy explained.

"I'm terribly sorry, but I don't know of anyone by either of those names."

She started to close the door, but Christy put her hand out to stop it.

"Please don't force me to call the police," the woman threatened.

"Karen, it's all right," another female voice called from within the house.

Karen opened the door wide, revealing a woman of approximately the same age. She too was immaculately dressed, but had kept her dark hair long. As she reached the door, Christy could see that the woman wore the matching wedding ring.

"I haven't been called by either of those names in what seems like a lifetime." Alison's voice cracked with emotion. "I'm Alison Willis now. Karen, please let me introduce you to my daughter."

Karen looked at Christy in surprise, then smiled warmly.

"Why don't you two go into the sitting room. I'm sure you have a few things to talk about." Karen said, gesturing for Christy to come inside. "I hope you can understand my earlier concern?"

"Of course," Christy said, tears threatening to pour down her face. "Do I need a mask?"

"No, you're alright," Karen replied. "I think it's fair to say that you qualify as part of our family bubble."

EPILOGUE

Paul stepped out of the shower and immediately heard the revving of a heavy-duty lawn mower coming from the front of the house. He had always intended to do the gardening himself when they finally found a house that required such a chore, but after his first attempt at trying to mow the lawn a few weeks previously, he had decided it was a task better left to the professionals.

Paul had spoken to Walter Brice, the manager of the local garden centre, about his lawn-care needs, and Walter had promised to bring around one of his lads to give the place a good trim. Then, if Paul liked what he saw, they could work out a price and make it a regular thing.

By the time Paul was dressed for another day of writing his latest manual – a rechargeable nose hair trimmer with a sideburn attachment – the front lawn was already well on the way to looking presentable. Walter Brice was looking on from the forecourt.

"Wow," Paul exclaimed. "He's doing a wonderful job."

"Aye, he is that," Walter replied, in his soft Highland accent. "He's new to the centre, but seems to know what he's doing."

Paul looked over at the young man. He was wearing

cargo shorts and a black t-shirt, even though the temperature was well below double figures, and seemed to sense Paul's gaze, for he turned to face him. Like many young men, he was sporting a full beard, yet Paul felt that he looked familiar.

Leaving the professionals to it, Paul headed inside for his morning cereal. The cutlery drawer was half open, and he felt a momentary jolt of adrenalin flood his system, until he saw that Christy had left a spoon sticking out, blocking the drawer from fully closing. He retrieved a spoon, then turned to the cupboard to grab a bowl and a box of Weetabix.

When he closed the cupboard door, he saw that the cutlery drawer was wide open again. He gently pushed it closed, not knowing what to think. There could not possibly be a third presence, could there?

Whilst he was internally debating the issue, the granite next to his breakfast things fogged over in a perfect circle. As he watched, two distinct dots appeared, then nothing else. Paul somehow knew it was his turn.

Then it dawned on him. He knew who the young gardener was.

It was Daniel.

As a smile broke across Paul's face, he added an upturned curved line to the fogged circle, completing the drawing.

He understood why Daniel had decided to stay.

BV - #0050 - 040522 - C0 - 197/132/15 - PB - 9781803780498 - Matt Lamination